FAMILIAR
DARKNESS

FAMILIAR DARKNESS

—a novel—

Evelyn Minshull

Baker Books

A Division of Baker Book House Co
Grand Rapids, Michigan 49516

Copyright © 1994 by Evelyn Minshull
Published by Baker Book House

Library of Congress Cataloging-in-Publication Data

Minshull, Evelyn White.
    Familiar darkness / Evelyn Minshull.
       p.   cm.
    ISBN 0-8010-6311-6
    I. Title
    PS3563.I476F35   1994
    813'.54—dc20   93-51260

For Kevin McQuiston
whose "dove" mural was also beautiful

I will give you the treasures of darkness,
   riches stored in secret places,
so that you may know that I am the Lord,
   the God of Israel, who summons you by name.
   —Isaiah 45:3

CHAPTER 1

We first saw our new parsonage in the angled beams of the pickup that had lumbered slowly ahead of us for sixty-plus miles of interstate and winding blacktop. Its headlights spotlighted the peeling door, once painted that green which distinguishes avocados and swamp slime. Massive gingerbread trim outlined the eaves with giant drools, like icing by a baker gone mad. It was the gingerbread that won me over; I could almost forgive Arden for having brought us to this godforsaken village just at a time when the city had seemed to offer everything I needed.

Though it was not godforsaken, Arden had insisted gently. After all, God was sending *us* here.

"It sure ain't much," the driver drawled. A darkly handsome man with deeply waved hair and narrowed eyes, he'd called himself Turk. The other, stouter man had introduced himself as Skinny.

"But then preachers don't expect much. Or shouldn't. You took them vows of poverty, right? And"—Turk's glance touched me briefly, speculatively—"chastity?"

Arden laughed.

It was the laugh, as melodious as his singing voice and as self-assured as his pulpit tones, that had warmed me as we courted and enclosed me with caring when I'd suffered my breakdown shortly after Pam's birth, two years ago.

"You've mangled the ecumenical lines, I'm afraid," he

said, his eyes crinkled with humor. "No, definitely not chastity, though poverty seems to have developed whether we vowed it or not." But there was no rancor in his words, only that deep, calm peace that steadied my soul when I was moderately calm, but frustrated and sometimes angered me when life pitched me about like a sailboat in a gale. How could he put up with me, I wondered. How could he endure the cold and flaring things I'd said, in unguarded moments, about coming here? The unrelenting silence I'd maintained throughout our trip?

As though reading my thoughts, Arden touched my arm, guiding me toward the wooden steps. "I'll be glad to explain the denominational differences, Turk, if you'd care to stop by some afternoon. Just now, we're very tired."

Turk dropped his cigarette onto the sidewalk, where it winked like an evil eye before extinguishing. "A man who *is* a man," he said, "don't need church."

If he realized that he'd insulted Arden, he didn't show it. Nor did Arden, who casually handed me the key for the front door and moved to wake Pam from her deep slumber in the backseat of our Chevy. Fritz, our terrier-mongrel, growled awake when Arden opened the car door.

Weariness of mind and body numbed the very marrow of my bones. I fumbled the key twice, then again as I heard Turk and Skinny heaving closer with the few furnishings we'd felt we'd need this first night. The movers would arrive with the rest tomorrow. My heart pounded in my ears. Tears crowded behind my eyes.

"Avoid fatigue, Paula," Dr. David had urged. "Stop two hours *before* you're tired, and you'll cancel eighty percent of your problems."

And I was four hours past fatigue. *God, help me*, I prayed, and then retracted the request. After all, the fatigue was God's fault. He was the one who had sent us here.

"Here." Skinny's massive hand closed over mine, extracting the key. He nudged me gently but firmly aside. "Little thing, ain't you?" He turned the key and the tumblers obeyed. "This town'll make mincemeat outa you." His matter-of-fact tone communicated only minimal sympathy.

Hear that, God?

The door creaked open. Blackness, flavored with the smell of fresh paint, rushed to meet me. I nearly asked Skinny not to turn on the lights. Blackness I was familiar with. Blackness on blackness on blackness. That had been the breakdown. Blackness above and around and within. Smooth blackness. Rough blackness. Clawing blackness. Smothering blackness. But, over and above it all, *familiar* blackness.

If only we could know just the darkness this first night. Sleep on the floor. Feel our way to the bathroom and around the fixtures. *Please.* I mouthed the silent words. *Please, no light—*

The lights startled a mouse in mid-floor. It stood galvanized for a moment, blinking; then, with a whiplike swirl of tail, skittered toward a pile of boxes and rags, surely remnants of recent cleaning.

But mouse feet are tiny, even when blurring with speed. With two bounds, Turk had overtaken it, raised one large booted foot directly over it, and—

No, I thought. No—

I could nearly feel the crunching of small bones.

Laughing, Turk turned to pin me with his dark eyes. "Good thing the carpet ain't laid yet," he said. "I'll take out the carcass for you. That spot ain't much ta clean up. Or just let the carpet cover it."

"You didn't need to—" I whispered harshly.

Skinny cleared his throat. "The lady's tired, Turk. You needn't have showed—quite that quick—what you are."

"Best she knows." His glance moved beyond me to the front doorway as Arden entered with Pam, sleepy-eyed and murmuring, draped in his arms like warm bread dough. They were so alike—her pale hair already hinting of auburn; Arden's deep tan nearly hiding the dusting of freckles high on his cheeks; her blue eyes a paler, wider imitation of his. Only her nose—turned up and tiny—and her tiptilted eyebrows mirrored me. Suddenly, intensely, I hated the thought of Turk's gaze touching Pam. A man who could crush a mouse that callously would surely hold a child in small regard. I stepped between him and Arden and eased Pam into my own arms. Warm, smelling of sleep and Fritz, she cuddled close.

"We'll get the cots in, ma'am," said Skinny, moving toward the door with ponderous steps. "Turk, clean up that mess and give me a hand. These folks need t'get t'bed."

Arden went with him, leaving Pam and me alone with Turk. Determined not to see the mouse again, I turned away. Every nerve balanced on edge, braced for what the man might say.

But he said nothing. And when he had followed the other two out, when I'd forced myself to look where the mouse had skittered and died . . . there was only one small spot of blood. But I knew that it would never truly lie hidden beneath the carpet. For me, that square inch of our new parsonage was already cursed by a callousness that could, as Skinny had forewarned, make mincemeat of me.

Chapter 2

The town had, in fact, made mincemeat of the past two ministers. We'd been made aware of this when Dr. Connelly, our district superintendent, first confirmed a transfer from the city church where Arden was assistant pastor.

The three of us had met in Arden's cubbyhole office. In a house, it would have been called a junk room, storing all manner of treasures too good or too full of memories to be discarded, but too battered or too out of style to be kept in use.

Stacked precariously along one wall were old pews, their worn seats and bruised legs bearing testimony to generations of shifting bodies and restless children, their ornately carved arms recalling a period when God had been worshiped in an aura of greater elaborateness, if not always of better taste.

A metal coatrack held shabby choir robes, once maroon in color. Dusty pyramids of boxes, undisturbed for decades, housed ancient hymnals, yellowed choir music, and Christmas cards unsold by Women's Societies long since inhabiting heavenly corridors.

Arden's office furniture suited its environment. A massive desk with carved, clawed legs and enough oak in its structure to build a dozen modern tables; three chairs (one overstuffed—horsehair beneath an ugly worn throw of tropical print; one heavy wooden folding chair with the name of

13

a defunct funeral home stenciled across the back; and the best one—where Arden had seated Dr. Connelly—a wheeled office chair of recent vintage, black and chrome). A sagging couch with crewel-worked cushions, three bookcases of varied sizes and styles, a ragged pseudo-Oriental rug, and a floor lamp that shot sparks whenever it was plugged in completed the decor.

I loved the place for its mismatched personality, so like my own. For its dusky paneled walls, reaching sixteen feet and further toward shadowed, vaulted timbers. And for the rich and unexpected spectrums and splotches of color cast by the slender stained-glass window, lending magic—even regality—to this place of dust motes and genteel decay.

"I don't want either of you to think," Dr. Connelly had begun that morning, his soft tones managing to sound both urgent and caring, "that the only reason you're moving is that this church has simply got to cut budget. Or that the only reason I've chosen you for the McClintock charge is that those three churches need a minister and you're available. The charge has problems, Arden. We need a strong man there." He paused, fidgeting with his glasses. "And a strong wife."

I fumbled with my wedding ring, turning it round and round, as I had in the hospital for hours on end.

"Paula is strong," Arden said firmly. He reached out, catching my hand, stilling my fingers with his.

Dr. Connelly cleared his throat. "Of course I know about the breakdown."

Of course, I thought. A mild anger stirred beneath the surface of my emotions. Even after only three years, I knew there was no privacy in the ministry, no way that a minister's wife could have a nervous breakdown, or even an attack of hives, without its becoming common knowledge within minutes.

"Then you know that she's better," Arden said. "She's strong enough to handle anything she needs to." The pressure of his fingers increased reassuringly.

"That's true," I said, and hated my voice for breaking.

"Then you're in favor of this move?" Dr. Connelly sounded as though, inwardly, he was drawing a deep sigh of relief. And why not? He had a problem charge, and he'd found someone to take it off his hands, at least for a year or two. He urged, "Paula . . . you're saying you want to go?"

But I wasn't saying that at all. "No."

He sighed. "You've heard, then, what happened with Winters."

Arden suggested mildly, "Suppose you tell us."

It wasn't a pleasant story. A minister, just a few years from retirement, driven from the church, from the ministry. His wife in a nursing home now, the victim of a stroke, not even recognizing their own children.

And the minister before that, a young man, now sold insurance.

My anger flared. "What's so special about McClintock that it deserves a human sacrifice every other year?"

Dr. Connelly straightened his tie, squirmed in his chair, and finally stood, striding about the cramped quarters, not looking at either of us.

If he says something sanctimonious, I thought, I'll have a tantrum, right on this fake Oriental rug. *Really* give him something to think about.

But he only shrugged, as though very tired. "I just don't know what makes a charge like that. Two of the three churches are fine. Always have been. Supportive. Caring. Enthusiastic. Growing." He sighed again. "It's something about the chemistry between the factions at McClintock, I suppose. And persistent suggestions of . . . impropriety. Some whispers, unsigned letters . . . nothing provable, apparently, but pervasive, nonetheless. Much as I hate to say it—what it needs is a good, clean church fight. And a split to clear the air. I've tried everything *I* can think of, heaven knows."

"And now it's our turn," I said quietly.

He turned to me then, and his eyes looked beaten. "But you said you didn't want to go—"

"I don't." It was my turn to stand, to pace. "I . . . I'm just beginning to like myself mornings, when I look in the mirror. I'm beginning to see myself as a worthwhile person. Someone who can contribute. I've even gone back for a master's degree."

Silence throbbed, pulsed, then closed down again. I imagined I could hear the settling of dust motes through that glorious, brilliant stream of multi-colored light that fell on the desk, on the rug, on my hands, spread as though to warm themselves.

I said, dully, "But Arden thinks that's what we ought to do."

"What we're called to do," Arden amended.

"Well!" Dr. Connelly straightened his shoulders and his smile. "*Well.* We've all been impressed with your ability to relate to people. Both of you. Maybe all McClintock needs is someone like the two of you. Someone who speaks the language of young people—"

"But they *had* a young minister. And now he's selling insurance."

He raised a reproving brow at me. "Young Martin was too soft for the ministry. Too insecure. Too . . . vulnerable." Catching up his briefcase, he shook Arden's hand, as though congratulating him on a promotion, rather than sentencing him to struggle and trauma. No. Not sentencing *him.* Sentencing *us.* "I'll tell them to expect you, then—the end of next month? Will that do? Give me a call in a day or two and we'll finalize. I can't tell you how pleased I am. Now, I really must hurry—"

And so the decision had been made. Not with Arden and me sitting down and talking it over, as we usually did. Yet not really arbitrarily either. Arden never had been one to "pull rank"; our marriage had always been a true partnership. But he was certain of this call. Sure that McClintock was where God wanted us to be, and that we needed this assignment as certainly as the three churches apparently needed us.

The sunshine that had begun to dispel my blackness—sunshine occasioned by my return to the university, by two or three growing friendships, by membership in a group of exhibiting artists—dissipated.

One rainy day, when Arden had gone on hospital visitation, I shut Fritz in the basement, bundled Pam into her slicker, gathered my paints, and went to the cubbyhole office. In the interim between early depression and the absolute inability to function, I had often huddled there. It was there I'd first thought of suicide as the only possible alternative—surely Arden and Pam would be better off without me. And it had been there, lying on the couch and staring numbly into rainbow-flecked cobwebs, that I'd determined to live.

Pam loved Arden's office, too. While rain liquefied the dulled colors of the stained glass, while I organized paint and brushes, she played with her doll among the pews, then curled up on the couch and went to sleep—thumb almost in her mouth, her jaws working as though the thumb were fully there, and her doll tucked beneath one flushed cheek.

I covered her with my coat and set up my easel.

My painting that day was easily the best I'd ever attempted. It captured the aura of majestic decay, reflected the warmth of the place, and evoked shadows of past confidences shared, past problems aired, and grievances healed. And, of course, it mirrored my love for the place and my pain at leaving it. I painted in acrylics; there would be no time for oils to dry before our move.

I knew that this painting would hang in our new parsonage, where I could see it every day . . . and remember.

CHAPTER 3

I hung the painting in an alcove where we would eventually place an easy chair and end table. Somehow, it belonged there. Its size was right for the space—not small enough to be overwhelmed, not large enough to dominate, and it was easily visible from the front doorway and all points of the living room. And the strange beige the Women's Society had chosen to repaint the room held overtones of peach, which echoed precisely the sun-warmed tones of the pews in the foreground.

After I'd hung it, Arden stood for long, silent moments, studying it. Then he reached out for me, and we stood, close together, remembering.

"I'm not sure I can bear to have it there," he said softly, "but I love it." His arm tightened around me. "You never wanted to leave, did you?"

I spoke past tears. "I could have grown roots there."

"But not branches," he said. "Taproots would have happened easily enough—had *already* happened. But there couldn't have been the reaching, and the growth pains." He patted me, dropping a kiss on my hair. "I love you for coming here with me."

I knew that I should respond with something as comforting, but the words wouldn't form. For I realized that, though the present moment murmured with warmth and peace, I was far from reconciled to a church that had mutilated the lives of its past two ministers and now surely waited, salivating, to see if it could destroy a third.

And then the moment had passed and I was preparing breakfast on the unfamiliar stove, while Arden set plastic picnic plates on the card table and caught the 7:00 o'clock news on our small portable TV set.

Our first visitors came while Pam was still sneaking syrup-soaked bits of pancake to Fritz, who knew as well as she did that he wasn't to be fed from any table and so greeted each tidbit with creditable surprise—eating it only, it seemed, to keep the floor tile inviolate. The visitors came to the kitchen door, rapping lightly, even as they peered through the screen.

That the two women were related was indicated by their large features, over-curled hair, and broad hand gestures that accompanied even the slightest remark. But there the resemblance ended. Margaret Pears was easily in her late sixties, yet she carried her large frame with a ramrod erectness that would have delighted any drill sergeant. White hair frothed about a pink face, and her teeth—which clicked punctuation for completed sentences—were even and white, though obviously ill-fitting. Not so her neat print dress, caught with a narrow belt and decorated with both a glittering pin and a draped silk scarf.

Like a quiet, bulky shadow, her granddaughter, Lelia, slumped in her wake—her dark hair an unruly tangle, her teeth in need of orthodonture. She seemed ill at ease in a long-sleeved blouse, tailored skirt, and black pumps.

"We wanted to be first," the older woman chattered. "We *are* first, ain't we?" She waved a hand in ornate acceptance of a folding chair and beamed at our assurance that they were, indeed, first. "Do call me Madge," she said. "All my friends call me Madge, and I'm *determined* that we shall be friends.

Lelia, sit down, dear. Yes, right over there, near the sweet, sweet child. If Mrs. Templeton allows, you may hold her. Might she, Mrs. Templeton?"

"Of course," I said. "And call me Paula."

"Was your father's name Paul, dear? Though you look Spanish, with those almond-colored eyes and high cheekbones. Paula's not really an *unheard*-of name, but unusual—unless the father's name was Paul. Lelia, here, was named for her father, Lee, who, unfortunately, chose not to wait around to see himself so honored."

I winced, an echo of the flinching in Lelia's muscles—a flinching she sought to hide by holding out a toy to Pam.

"Lelia's a lovely name," I said, trying some camouflage of my own. "So . . . delicate." And so unfitting, I thought, for such a utilitarian face and body. And yet Lelia's smile was lovely, despite the teeth, as relaxed-at-last she continued her play with Pam.

"Lelia baby-sits." A spiral flourish of Madge's hand denied the possibility of hinting. "Poor girl, she's busy more nights than she's not, giving her absolutely *no* time for friends or dating."

Lelia's fingertips froze on the edge of the table, and Pam battered at them gleefully with a dripping spoon.

"She likes you," I said, removing the spoon from Pam's stubborn grasp.

The smile was stiff at first, then warming. "Children always seem to."

"Because you like *them*." I resisted the urge to touch her arm. "Children and dogs can always tell." Fritz yipped, happy to be a part of the conversation at last.

"Down." Pam dimpled at Lelia. "Pam wants down."

"Then *get* down." Arden shook his head slightly at Lelia, who seemed perfectly willing to gather our grubby little girl into her arms. "Then go wash your hands and maybe you could show Lelia around the house. Or—" he laughed, "she could show you."

Madge chuckled. "There's truth in that! She stayed nights, often, with poor Mrs. Winters, before she got so bad. And did the bulletins for young Andy Martin. And the Smiths, before that." Her hands performed somewhat-symmetrical patterns. "This parsonage has been a second home to Lelia from the time she could toddle. Though that don't seem so long. How the years *do* scoot by! That little one—" she nodded after Pam and Lelia, "she'll be breathing heavy after boys before you've turned around twice. That's the way of the flesh. *And* the law of God," she amended hastily, casting an awkward glance toward Arden. "God made them two and two, ain't that right, Reverend, and ordered them to get on with replenishin' the earth. Why, I was doing my part, bearing her mother, long before I was Lelia's age. And six more, past her. All married young, themselves."

She sighed ponderously. "I do worry about Lelia some, but put it down to her father leaving when she was no more than three-quarters made. And of course her mother—" She hitched about in her chair, her hands still for just those seconds, but taking renewed flight as she continued her story. "She never *did* recover. From her bitterness, you know. Never married again, though she had plenty o' chances. Never had a good word to say for a man since—'*less* he was a man of the cloth, Reverend. A breed set apart, as God's Word says."

"'A peculiar people'?" Arden asked, his laughter thinly disguised.

She hesitated. "Well . . . some *think* it peculiar, ministers bein' above and beyond the lusts of common man. Or should be, though there *was* some talk about . . . well!" She stood firmly, giving neither of us time to react. "I'll be off. There's two more visits before 'The Flame and the Fury' comes on.

You watch that, do you, Paula? Though I s'pose not, being a minister's wife. There is a lot of S - E - X and all, but it's true to life, I swear it is. I can see myself in Dianna, though I never had but the two husbands, and she's had four, and is on trial for murder of this last one, though goodness knows he deserved it. The *picture* of Lee! I couldn't believe when I saw him on the screen that first time. I knew then he was up to no good, just out for his own lustful pleasure—and her so sweet and trusting. Though you'd wonder how she still could be after all those men—not just the ones she was married to, you understand. But I saw him and knew he couldn't look that much like Lee and not be like Lee—"

"Oh, Lelia!" I interrupted, as she returned to the kitchen. She'd removed the pumps, I noticed. "Did Pam show you her toy box? I'm surprised you escaped so quickly!"

"I was wondering." Her hands flew at sharp angles, then clasped before her. "I was wondering—since you haven't finished moving in—if you'd like me to watch her today. I—I mean, no charge—"

"That's very kind." Arden's words, soft and warming, did their work.

Lelia's hands unclasped and dropped to her sides. She drew a deep sigh. "I know you must have a lot to do—"

Madge had obviously been quiet for as long as was bearable. "And here *I* stand, chattering away, keepin' you from it! I meant to bring you a cake or a loaf of bread, but Liz Sweitzer'll do that—she always does—and thinks nobody can bake t'match her, so I let her think it. Now, Lelia, you remember to get home by five. Tonight's Bingo night. And you, Paula and Reverend, if she gets in your way, just send her home. We never was ones to wish our children on the neighbors." Never missing a beat of her monologue, she was out the door, down the back steps, and well down the sidewalk before near-silence filled the gap she had left.

We stood, unmoving, until Pam dropped a toy on the floor in the living room.

Lelia, her face a study in embarrassment, twisted her hands. "I'm . . . twenty-two," she said helplessly.

I did touch her arm then. "Maybe, in the eyes of our parents and grandparents, we never really grow up."

With a look of almost pathetic gratitude, she went to rejoin Pam.

CHAPTER 4

By mid-afternoon the movers had come. So had Liz Sweitzer, with a loaf of bread still warm through its wrapping—a calendar towel, grown soft with use in the five years since its prime; a sweeper salesman; Ellie and Kelly Anderson, eight-year-old twins, to see if we had any children their age; a teenager selling magazine subscriptions; and Mrs. Campbell, from next door, assuring us that she was easy to get along with and had never had any trouble with any of the former pastors, despite the fact that she was herself a Baptist and didn't quite trust anyone who scarcely got sprinkled instead of being thoroughly and decently dunked.

In the next breath, she expressed concern that we not only had Fritz, we also had Pam. "I don't mind, of course. Everyone knows dogs and children are necessary evils. Just do please tell them both that my glads take prizes at the fair every year."

As a gesture of goodwill, she gave me her recipe for apple butter. "I've never made it, but Grandmother did, and it was excellent. Though I've never cared much for apple butter myself."

Neither had Arden and I, but I thanked her anyway and promised that both Pam and Fritz would respect boundaries. And gladioli.

By early evening, the kitchen was beginning to feel familiar, with our own clock on the wall—quartz, the shape of an orange slice; our cheery plates on the sideboard; our dented toaster, ready to be plugged in; and, near the doorway, our throw rug, crocheted by a dear old soul I would never forget—though I realized, with some panic, that already the warm, wrinkled lines of her face were softening in my memory, smudged by too many new impressions. Even the stove, called on to heat coffee or tea water for most of our visitors that afternoon, was no longer a stranger.

If I could stay in the kitchen, I thought, clearing up after supper, I could believe I was back where I longed to be, except for the sleepy murmur of nesting birds in the big tree outside the window. That sound evoked memories of childhood trips to my grandparents' farm.

But beyond the kitchen, the house was, if not hostile, at least not yet receptive. Our TV, playing softly for Pam and Fritz, had not transformed the living room. Our blue-covered couch hadn't taken kindly to the Women's Society's strange beige paint. Even my painting was all too stark a reminder that we'd brought with us only the replica, not the reality, of belongingness. And though I'd placed another throw rug strategically, the memory of the crushed mouse was still vivid, as I'd feared it would be.

Straighten up, Paula, I told myself sternly. This is the stuff depressions are made of.

I shuddered. Clawing out of the blackness, such a short time before, I'd promised myself that never would I endure a second descent into that dark hell. When I'd felt myself slipping, at times, with each small backward sliding I'd tasted again the terror, the starkness, the alienation.

That moment, my hands in the chilling dishwater, I experienced it again.

Please, God . . . You brought us here.

Or had He?

I'd often envied the certainty of the answers to biblical

prayers. And yet Gideon had placed the *second* fleece. Even then, so close to the presence of God, His people had questioned. How much more did *our* generation—separated by distance, time, and technology, by a zillion arguments and reinterpretations, by centuries of questioning and chaos—find definitive answers difficult.

I was so deep in these thoughts that the noise intruded itself slowly—only another thread of sound woven in the tapestry of the settling birds, the murmuring TV, the creakings of the house, the soapsuds dying around my stilled hands.

But once I'd caught it, my alerted senses focused, tuning out all else. There was a scraping. A grating. A creaking. And . . . voices? And then the unmistakable tinkling of shattering glass.

"Hey!" The voice was intense but young.

I moved to the outside kitchen door and opened it cautiously, just to the point where I could see past the corner of the parsonage, past the length of the annex housing Sunday school rooms, to the side entrance of the sanctuary. Within the church itself some light source ignited stained glass with flickering tongues of color.

I stepped onto the back porch, which creaked beneath my weight. Its three steps ended in broken sidewalk I'd walked often enough that day to remember. Fronds of unkempt forsythia stroked me as I passed the looming annex. Beside it, broken glass lay glittering, just faintly, on the pavement.

Suddenly, I wished I'd called for Arden. I'd thought he was outside, walking the grounds or investigating the church. But he might be upstairs in the house, in the room that would be his study. Or even napping.

Youth gave no guarantee of innocence or friendliness. Almost daily in the media, horror stories verified that fact.

Remembering young gangs that had roamed even our peaceful part of the city, I turned back toward the parsonage, away from the trouble.

But only briefly.

From within the church I heard the thud of something heavy and the screech of ripping wood. Glass crunched beneath my feet as I moved toward the threshold.

Once I entered the building, I had no idea what I'd do next. But there was no need for strategy. Suddenly the sanctuary blazed with overhead light. Four boys, none older than ten or eleven, swung in a startled unit to face Arden, who stood beside the light switches, beyond the tiers of pews.

As he moved down the carpeted aisle toward them, they shrank together. One clutched a baseball bat. I could see the thumping of the pulse at his temple. Another tightened his grip on a claw hammer. A third fumbled a spray paint can, eventually holding it behind him.

"Let's get outta here," one growled, and the group unfroze, only to re-solidify as they found me in their way.

Like Fritz when he was scolded, they crumpled. Eyes suddenly wide, empty of bravado, shoulders hunched forward, they epitomized vulnerability.

So young, I thought. Mischievous, but not street-wise. Not tough enough yet to put up a front and turn their fear against the feared. Except for one.

In the time it had taken Arden to reach the front pew and pause there, looking at the boys in turn, this one had changed. Arrogance was evident in the tightening of muscles, in the raised eyebrow and the "I-dare-you" firmness of his mouth.

Watch that one, I thought.

Arden motioned for the boys to sit down, and they did. All but the one.

Arden leaned against the communion rail. "It was nice of you guys to come by," he said.

Three of the boys started, then relaxed a little.

"Who ya kiddin'?" sneered the one standing. "Creep."

Arden let that pass.

"Aw, Dean," grumbled the smallest boy—the one with the bat. He was a frail boy, with bony wrists and fragile shoulders. The pulse still throbbed in his temple, but more slowly. His eyes, pale blue, were fringed with long dark lashes that fluttered against unbelievably pale skin. The tanned bulk of the other three underlined his frailty.

Dean snarled, "We shoulda left chicken-guts *Tim-o-thy* playin' checkers with his sister!"

The frail boy's cheek twitched.

"Lay off him," said a freckled boy with wild dark hair and a Band-Aid across the bridge of his nose. "Ain't we in trouble enough?"

"Trouble?" Dean asked airily. "We ain't in no trouble! You heard the parson say it himself. We just dropped by t'call. T'wish him a good year at McClintock."

"And to ask him to paint your baseball bat I suppose," I said, more to myself than to them.

Dean spoke over his shoulder. "Dry up, lady."

"Aw, Dean—"

"And dry up, *Tim-o-thy*."

"How 'bout 'Dry up, *Dean*'?" It was the boy with the can of spray paint who'd spoken. He was taller than Dean, with the lean, clean look of an athlete, and—now that he'd relaxed—an evidence of self-esteem in his eyes. "Why don't we quit kiddin', Dean? We all know why we're here. And so do they."

Tim shuddered. The freckled boy braced himself against the back of the pew. Dean turned his scornful glance on each of them, but they were watching Arden.

I could almost feel sorry for Dean—the leader without a group to lead. Clearly, the others planned to throw themselves upon the mercy of the court. They seemed to be waiting only for Arden to pronounce sentence.

But Arden just stood there, waiting quietly.

Silence stretched in the muffled shifting of feet, the measure of deep-drawn sighs, the creaking of the pew, the distance-dimmed sounds from beyond the gaping door. A moth fluttered in and honed its flight toward the pulpit light. I closed the door, but another moth sailed through the ruptured pane.

"Hey, mister," the freckled boy began, finally.

"Rev," Tim corrected. "I seen it on the sign out front. Rev Arden Templeton. That's what it said."

Arden's eyes twinkled. "That's short for 'Reverend,' Tim," he said. "But 'mister' is fine."

The freckled boy swallowed. "Yeah. Thanks. It's just . . . I was gonna say . . . we wasn't gonna do much. And the glass—well, that was an accident. The door stuck."

"I noticed, this afternoon. Paula, honey, remind me to fix that tomorrow."

"Yeah. Well. We'll pay for the glass. And the—" He glanced nervously toward the choir loft, and I noticed that one of the ornate posts was broken. "That—" he swallowed again. "That—wasn't an accident."

New silence followed this confession.

When Dean finally spoke again, his voice broke. "You guys make me sick, ya know that? You spill your guts t' this—this city *pansy* here—and what's he gonna do? What's he gonna *do?*"

The fear was in their eyes again.

"Well," Arden finally said, stepping away from the communion rail, "the first thing I'm going to do is see how we can repair this post here." He moved to the choir loft and looked closely at the broken post. "Paula, could you bring me the toolbox . . . some glue . . . that can of plastic wood?"

Tim was off the pew, baseball bat laid aside, scrunching down beside Arden to peer at the post—his paleness intensified by Arden's tan and auburn coloration. "Won't it show where you mend it?"

"Where *we* mend it," Arden corrected.

Tim frowned, clearly not understanding. "Yeah, well. Dad says t'use a C-clamp or something. 'Course, how would ya get a C-clamp on *that?*"

"A very good question," Arden said. "Next time you break something, you need to consider that." He glanced at me, and I remembered what he'd asked me to do. I needed to check on Pam, too, I chided myself as I hurried to the rear of the sanctuary, then through the annex toward the parsonage. Some mother I was. I'd totally forgotten that she and Fritz were alone in the house.

The living room was much too quiet. Though the TV still chattered and sang, there were no answering giggles from Pam. My heart lurched as I saw her spot on the throw rug empty and then—the front door standing open.

"Pam!" It was a frozen whisper. "Pam!"

Almost at once I heard the patter of Fritz's footsteps on the porch, then Pam's grunting as she lifted her short legs laboriously up the steps.

"Pam! Honey—"

"Lady comed." She pattered, smiling, toward me, extending a half-eaten ginger cookie. "Nice lady."

"But—" I held her close, so close that she wriggled to be free. "Where is she? The lady?"

She flopped down, engrossed again with the TV.

I was worrying needlessly, I told myself. Outside, sleepy night sounds murmured. Nothing evil there, surely. Still, I hurried to close the door, making sure it was locked—and knowing with trembling certainty that it had been locked before. Then how . . . ?

I'd left the kitchen door open when I'd gone to the church. Swiftly I closed and locked it, too—trying not to wonder how many of the members might have keys.

It was nothing. Just as Pam had said, a "nice lady" had given her a cookie. Fritz certainly hadn't seemed suspicious. Of course, Fritz rarely did! I peered out the window, studying shadows. One seemed to detach itself from a tree trunk and move away. Perhaps just the breeze moving the leaves?

Nevertheless, I took Pam with me when I returned to Arden with the things he'd requested.

CHAPTER 5

The way it works," the tall, blond checkout clerk said as she rang up apples, rolls, eggs, and margarine, then pressed the button to move the array down to the bag boy, "is that they lay out the red carpet first. Liz Sweitzer'll bring by some bread. Has she already?"

I nodded.

"Mmmmm, *mmmmm*," she murmured, with more than slight satisfaction. "There'll be Jell-O salads, pies, cakes, and advice. Most of all, advice. And Tara Campbell will be sure t'let you know that Baptists and glads make the best neighbors."

I smiled.

"So that's happened already, too." She peered at me over her glasses and rang up the pork chops. "I'm Skinny's wife."

It took a moment for that to register.

"Oh! Yes. We really appreciated his help, getting some of our things moved in for the first night."

"His pleasure." She rang up detergent and cheese. "Skinny's not much of a church man. He'll be there Sunday, though. So will a lot of other folks you'll never see again. Just t'sorta check things out. See if your husband says what they want t'hear." She paused, posting the price of milk. "Not necessarily what they *need* t'hear. What they *want* t'hear."

Another pause as the bananas slid down the incline

toward the waiting bag. "And they'll check *you* out, too. Skinny said they wouldn't like you." She pressed the button for tax, precipitating a series of beeps and rattles. "They like a minister's wife plain. Faded and dowdy, as befits a pious woman—makes *them* look better. They'd be pleased, too, if you could put on twenty pounds or so, mostly around the middle."

We exchanged smiles, and I found myself liking her very much. Just as I'd liked Skinny.

"Dora Kuhn." She extended her hand. Her clasp was firm, as I'd thought it would be. "That's me. I'll be there—in the choir. And in charge of coffee at the reception, after." Grinning, she stamped my check. "Just don't think the reception's t'make you feel at home. It's for the ones who didn't have a good view during church. Besides, they can grade you on table manners and see how you manage your little girl."

Leaning forward, she said, "Oh, there'll be all sorts of goodies there. Everybody brings her best recipe—trying to impress each other. But good food serves a lot of purposes. Puts people off guard, for one thing. Makes them sluggish. Just remember, they fatten up the calf, too—just before the kill."

Though Madge Pears had said, when she told us about the reception, that it wasn't necessary for us to take anything, Lelia later confided that some of the women had never forgiven Mrs. Winters for showing up without a casserole.

"Take table service, too," she advised, her hands twitching nervously, her newly washed hair like an untidy dark aura about her head. "If you don't have time to fix something, I'll be glad to. But . . ." her eyes filled with tears, "it *hurt* Rev. Winters!"

I felt a rush of warmth for Lelia. As old as she was, she was still a sensitive, vulnerable child.

I touched her arm. "I have a pepper-potato recipe that's a real crowd-pleaser," I said, "and it's easy to make. But thanks."

"I . . . I want you to like it here. I just couldn't stand it when the Winters left. And before that—" She swallowed noisily.

I turned away, frowning. Here was a by-product of the divided church too often skimmed over. Always I'd felt sympathy for the minister. But there were other victims. Many people required a sturdy church fellowship. Needed to know that there was someone in the parsonage who shared enough common knowledge of the recent past that he—or she—could speak with both the authority of God's Word and the caring of a trusted friend.

Arden had been reaching that place of trust with the people of our old church.

I tasted bitterness at the thought.

We could have stayed there. Grown old there. Felt those roots we had mentioned reaching down and out, giving strength to the place and gaining strength from it.

Lelia said softly, "I know you don't like it here."

Ashamed, I turned. "It's just that we loved it where we were. It's not that we aren't learning to . . . care for you."

And it was true, I realized. Pam, especially, was forming a warm bond with Lelia, readily offering her love, as children do. And Arden and I had discussed Lelia's obvious need for self-esteem. She was scarcely five years younger than I. Yet I was beginning to worry about her more as though she were Pam's older sister than a parishioner we'd known for only a few days.

"I . . . think I'll go home now," Lelia said. She fumbled her chair back in place. "When Pam wakes up, if you need me, I could take her to the park."

Later, I took advantage of Arden's preoccupation with his sermon notes, while Pam and Fritz played on a blanket nearby, to go sketching.

All week we'd been so busy settling in, so concerned with fitting into niches worn by others and making ourselves and our furniture seem to belong, that there'd been no time to explore farther than the grocery store on mid-Main Street, opposite the park, and the post office on the corner of Main and Bank Streets.

Now I finally had time to walk up Walnut Avenue to Bridgemont, past the senior citizen housing and on to the woods, contained by straggling wire fence incapable of restraining a chipmunk, much less the Angus bulls it had once enclosed, according to Lelia.

Stepping over the looped and useless wire, I entered the woods slowly.

Sunlight, filtered through shifting foliage, cast Morse code splashes of brilliance indiscriminately—sometimes highlighting gentians, dogtooth violets, and moss-covered rocks, or, just as often, nothing more beautiful than last autumn's leaves, decayed to mush.

A walk in any woods always thrilled and soothed me. Much as I'd loved the city, at times my soul had cried for the quietude, the beauty, of woodland. But there'd been only the park, and—crazily—the mall. When I desperately needed plants and flowers, a place to think with at least the appearance of solitude, I'd often hurried to the mall's center, hiding myself near the coin-littered waterfall, with the bustling world of shoppers shut out by drooping philodendron leaves and sprays of palm.

Both before my depression had become insufferable and after my hospitalization, when terror had begun to lessen, Arden had often found me there.

"Little girl, Paula," he'd teased, but with tension clouding his eyes and his voice, "couldn't you come talk to me when you're troubled?"

"I needed to talk to *God.*"

"And did you find Him here?"

A stiffening in my throat. "Don't you think I could?"

"Of course you could!" His voice muffled as he held me close. "When He walked the desert and spoke from a mountaintop . . . when He whispers through summer breezes and sings through the throat of a nightingale . . . why should a mall be impossible?"

"I . . . feel so silly is all. When you find me here."

"Would you rather I didn't look for you?" There was pain in his tone.

"No! No. I *need* you to find me, I think—just as much as I need to come here."

"Then come as often as you like—as often as you must."

"They look at me strangely sometimes."

"The shoppers?"

"No. They're too busy hunting bargains. The children. They see me."

"They'd probably like to join you in here!"

"I feel childlike here. Like I'm hiding in my secret place. Did you have one, ever? I guess everyone does! I need one now. And the mice look at me strangely, too."

"Mice?" Tension melted into quiet laughter. "You mean mice dare live *here*, in the shadow of Lafite's Boutique and the V.P. Lounge?"

"It's because of the lounge they're here. I saw one nibbling on ham today. And another—I think—had lobster."

"Well, at least they're mice of good taste!"

"I've always rather liked mice. Field mice, especially. I remember Grandad unrolling snow fence once, and there were two tiny ones, hardly as big as his thumb, standing there near his boot. Not the least bit frightened."

"He didn't—"

"Kill them? I could never have forgiven him if he had. He picked them up, very gently, in those huge gloved hands and carried them to another snow fence."

A pause. Then, "Are you ready to go home with me now, honey? I'll make you some cocoa."

"Oh, Arden . . . oh, Arden . . . " The tears beginning, strength gone from knees and hands. "How . . . can you ever bear—"

"Shhhhh. I love you, now more than ever. Let's go home, love. Let's go home."

As the scene replayed in my memory, I worked my way into heavy woodland.

Tears blurred my vision—those tears that always came when such memories claimed me. But they were quiet tears. Calm tears. Tears of gratitude that God had indeed spoken from such places as the rainbowed church office and the botanical garden in the mall. Gratitude that Arden had loved me. Still loved me.

I found a large flat rock that might have been hewn by a giant. It crested a slope, overlooking a small dell partitioned by a dry streambed, now crisscrossed by rampant vine and bramble.

Opening my sketchbook, I began a pencil detail of leaf pattern.

Engrossed, I worked until neither the shafts of sunlight nor their warmth penetrated the deep-layered foliage. No one knew where I was, and Arden would be expecting to help me make dinner. Suddenly, I felt alone. Separated. Vulnerable.

Whether that tremor of isolation came first, or whether it followed the feeling that I was being watched, I couldn't have said with certainty. There is a certain "hangover"—a dullness, a suspension between worlds—that bridges my deepest concentration on a sketch and my return to reality. It was through that dullness that the awareness filtered. A spine-crawling certainty that someone—something?—was watching me.

Perhaps a squirrel, I thought, turning slowly—wanting, yet not wanting, to see my observer. Or a domestic animal. A cat. A dog out for a stroll.

"Is someone there?" I called, tentatively, feeling foolish in the event there was no one there; feeling even more foolish if there were.

There was no answering stir of leaves, no footstep, no hearty "Hello." Nothing. Yet the certainty deepened. And it was no animal, I was sure by then, that brought the shivering to my neck, the rapidity to my heartbeat.

Often, feeling this way in the hospital, I had turned, frightened, to find myself pinioned beneath the gaze of a nurse or a doctor taking notes. There was that impersonal aura to the feeling now. Nothing of warmth in the observation of which I was the subject.

No hostility either?

Perhaps not. Just—more chilling, even, than hostility—an apathy. I was of no more importance to the observer than an amoeba on a microscope slide.

Or—a mouse under a heavy boot?

Gathering my things with more haste than effectiveness, I chided myself. Turk had come to mind simply because I'd been thinking about mice in the mall . . . about Grandad and the field mice. Still, feeling once again the horror of tiny bones crunching, I hurried toward the remaining light at the edge of the woods. And all across the open field, I never lost the sensation that I was being watched.

CHAPTER 6

I couldn't sleep.

Trying to breathe quietly, to turn over in bed without disturbing Arden, I felt the minutes move ponderously past. I checked the illuminated dial of the alarm clock with what seemed like disciplined infrequency but averaged out at every four minutes.

When I was in the hospital, there'd been nights like this when I'd managed to sneak my sleeping pills under the pillow or into the pocket of my robe for later disposal—or, at one crucial period, for hoarding, in the event that I'd need them all at once. When Arden had brought Pam for a short visit, my hand had strayed there, clenched them. Crushed them. Later, I'd emptied my pocket over the commode and flushed it firmly.

Once I'd been discharged, I tried to make certain each night that I was weary enough for sleep, for the demons of lonely awakeness were more demoralizing than all the shadows of fear and worry that could dog my days.

It was in that quiet darkness that I paid homage to ancient guilts and future fears. It was then that I replayed small scenes. Vivid, stark, and numbing. The afternoon, obscenely sunny, when my father's casket sat drowned in wilting flowers that fluttered only faintly in the breeze; when my mother, spent with sadness, sat dull-eyed, beyond feeling, and my sister flirted with a distant cousin. The day when, very young, I'd been accused by my teacher of tracing a drawing, and I'd stamped my foot and been sent down long, echoing corridors to the principal's office. The time after time after time when I'd tried to force my older, godlike brother to notice me, and he hadn't. Ever. The day I learned that the girl I'd never liked had been shot by her brother as he was cleaning his gun. And that some of her blood and brain had spattered her open social studies book.

Over and over, behind clenched eyelids, the scenes played—my sister's whispers and light laughter distorting to blend in a grim cacophony with the thud of a bullet into a young girl's brain and my embarrassing demand for attention I never received.

My leg cramped, and I moved stiffly to ease it. Arden's arm came over me heavily; he murmured something the texture of overcooked rolled oats.

And it was scarcely midnight.

I could not, I would not make it to morning. Not at this pace, more sluggardly than limping snails.

Easing from beneath Arden's arm, I felt for my robe and slippers and squeaked on tiptoe across the floor that had seemed sturdy and silent enough by daylight.

Fritz met me just outside the bedroom door, and we crept downstairs together.

At the foot of the stairs, remembering the flimsiness of our curtains and a figure that might or might not have been watching from deeper tree shadow, I resisted turning on a light.

Anyway, what could I do between then and morning? Bake? Sew? The noise would waken Arden and Pam. Read a book? Most of mine weren't unpacked yet, and I didn't feel up to the heavy reading between fake leather covers on Arden's shelves.

Paint?

Perhaps. Later. But, just for a bit, I'd sit in the darkness, gathering it about me like a blanket. Sleep might prove less reluctant there.

At my knee, Fritz whined, jostling me. Then, impatient, he moved to the door—not the front door, his exit for a run, but the one connecting parsonage living room and annex.

"No, Fritz," I whispered. "Here." Dragging myself from the couch, I padded to the front door. "Here, boy."

Whining, he remained where he was.

"Here!"

Intensifying, the whine threatened to erupt into a bark.

Sighing, I gave in. I'd have to take him through the annex, proving that for once I knew more than he did. Then, maybe he'd condescend to leave by the front door.

The annex door opened quietly. Arden, once he'd replaced the glass in the side church door and eased its opening, had made the rounds with oil for all balky hinges.

"There," I whispered. "Are you satisfied?"

But light glowed, past the kitchen fixtures, from the Sunday school rooms, partitioned by sliding vinyl room dividers like rigid drapes.

And there was sound. A swishing. An occasional rattling.

Like paint from a spray can!

I bent to pet Fritz, both as apology and as request for quietness, and we moved softly together toward the light, toward those sounds.

Even before we saw him, I knew that it would be Dean.

This time he was alone. And too involved with his work to have noticed us.

It was all I could do to choke down a shout. If I frightened him, though, heaven only knew what his reflexes might accomplish. Already, the rough-plastered wall, fresh-painted eggshell, was decorated with a wild design in black enamel. By staying quiet for a moment longer, perhaps I could save the ceiling, the piano, furniture, floor, and dividers.

Fritz padded on alone, and Dean, turning, set down the spray can and bent to tickle him behind the ears. I forced myself to stand still in the shadows until my breathing had steadied, until my thoughts had eased to a simmer. And while I waited, I studied the damage, wondering how we could ever get the wall restored in just the one day that lay between us and Sunday morning.

Despite the fact that my mind was tired—or perhaps because of it—I noticed, emerging from the erratic sprayings, a pattern. A design. The bone structure of a mural. Crazy as it was, excitement infiltrated dismay and began to take over.

Just then Fritz whined toward me, and Dean looked around. One hand grew rigid in the dog's fur, twisting it; the other reached for the spray can. Holding it like a grenade at the ready, Dean straightened slowly.

I moved toward him, suppressed excitement throbbing through my words. "Do you have any idea what you've *done?*"

"What we come to do the other night." Swallowing loudly, he leveled the spray can. "Don't come near me, lady!"

"But look at it! Really *look* at it!"

His lip curled. "Oh, sure. Then you sneak up and grab—"

"Don't be silly! I'm not interested in grabbing you! What would I do with you if I caught you?" I forced a calmer tone. "Just look at what you've drawn on the wall."

His expression wobbled. I watched him fighting himself, wanting to look but needing to keep me at bay. And then he yawned widely. Such a childlike yawn.

"Don't worry," I said gently. "I promise I won't try to capture you. Just look, please look, at the design you've made."

"But . . . I didn't mean to make no design."

"Sometimes, they're the very best kind." I nodded encouragement. "Look."

He did, then shook his head. "I was just tryin' t'cover as much of the wall as possible. So it would take weeks t'clean it off."

"What would you say if . . . if we *didn't* clean it off?"

"Not—" He stared at me. "You're crazy, lady! You know who goes to this church? A lotta people who can't stand a speck of dust, let alone a mess like this." He turned, looking again, shrugging again.

"You really don't see it, do you?" I asked. "The descending dove?"

"The *what* dove?"

"Descending. It's a symbol. Of the Holy Spirit."

No sign of recognition lit his eyes. And, clearly, he was fighting another yawn.

"Remember when the Spirit of God descended on Jesus when He was being baptized? It came in the form of a dove."

"Even if I did—"

"There," I said, and moved forward.

Just for an instant he stiffened, ready for battle or flight. I paused until he'd relaxed, allowing me to stand beside him; then I traced, not touching, the wide, free wings, spread triumphantly. Showed him the head, even the eye. The light shafted downward from clustered clouds.

"Yeah," he admitted. "Maybe. But it don't make no difference. You'll hafta clean it off. Or *he* will." He gave me a conspiratorial glance. "It was him I really meant to get to. He thought he was so cool, leanin' there, showin' we couldn't bother him." He nodded toward the wall. "I figured *this*'d bother him!"

I smiled. "You could be right."

"Only the other guys wouldn't come. They say they like him. But I know they're just chicken."

"He's a very likeable guy," I said.

"Yeah. Sure. You hafta say that!"

"Who'd make me?"

He just shrugged, covered another yawn, and oozed down on the floor, his back against the wall. Fritz wriggled over, laying his head on the boy's crossed knees.

"So," he asked, "what're we gonna do?"

I paused, weighing probable repercussions.

I'd done church murals before, but never without commission. Or at least permission! Even in a church that nourished ministers and thus might forgive what passed for presumption, what I hoped to do would be taking a calculated risk. And here at McClintock, well . . .

Well, God, You brought us here—right? At least Arden feels so. And if You did, it must have been for a reason—not just to have us mangled, too. And You brought this boy here, on a night when Fritz and I couldn't sleep.

With startling clarity, Mordecai's charge to Esther ignited my memory. "And who knows whether you have not come to the kingdom for such a time as this?" At least I wouldn't risk execution for my rashness!

"We're going to finish it," I said, and shivered. Dean just sat there, staring, while I moved to the wall and touched the paint gingerly. "Fast dry?" I asked.

He nodded. "Alcohol base." He cleared his throat. "I wanted it t'be good and set when he found it."

"We'll use latex. For the color."

"You really mean this, don't ya?"

"I really mean it." I felt new purpose gather. "I really do! Look, why don't you clean up those speckles on the floor? I'll get newspapers and the paint, and we'll see how much we can finish by morning."

I wondered if he might take this opportunity for escape. But he was waiting there, his eyelids drooping, when I

returned with remnants of latex left over from my most
recent mural.

"Let me show you how I think it might be done." I
began sketching rapidly on a margin of newspaper. "If you
don't like it, say so. It's your Sistine Chapel."

"What's a Sis—"

"Never mind. Just watch."

I visualized the mural as semi-abstract, making maxi-
mum use of his free-wheeling lines, which could outline and
segment, much like lead in a stained glass window. Color
would be applied abstractly, further delineating shape, while
the eggshell hue, untouched, would do for lighter areas of
dove breast and wing tip, light shaft, and highlighted cloud.

"Three blues, I think," I said, and showed him. "Several
grays. A touch of rose at beak and eye and claw—and the
same color, lightened, just warming the cloud tones."

"I like it!" he said. "Can . . . can I help?"

"No," I said, and explained quickly to dispel his frown of
disappointment, "I'll help. If you don't mind."

"Heck, no! I've never done a whole wall before." And he
added quickly, "Not one to keep."

We worked quietly for hours, communicating by glance
and murmur, and swiftly cleaning up small messes when
slightly wet enamel smudged or latex dripped to linoleum.

At last, too tired for thought, I made hot chocolate in the
church kitchen. Sitting on the floor, we sipped it carefully,
while Fritz divided his attention between us.

"Shouldn't we call your folks and let them know where
you are?" I asked, wondering why the thought hadn't
occurred to me before.

"Naw. I live with my Gramma, and she never knows
when I go out."

I thought that one over thoroughly, through a long
silence punctuated by blowing and sipping.

"You know," he said levelly, "you're weird."

"So I've been told."

He raised his eyebrow. "Yeah. Well . . . ya just don't act right."

"Oh?"

"Like t'night. Ya shoulda—"

"Yes?"

"Well, I guess there are a lotta things ya coulda done. Like (a)—ya coulda yelled, like my ol' man when he was home."

"It takes a lot to make me yell."

"This ain't a lot?"

I had to smile.

"And (b)—ya coulda cried, like my Gramma."

"I don't know you well enough to be disappointed in you."

He considered that before hitting (c). "I even thought ya might call the cops."

"And if I had?"

"I'd've run like—" He caught his lower lip between his teeth.

"But I know your name."

"Not my last one." Taking a long sip of chocolate, he watched me over the rim of his cup.

"Fair enough," I said. "But how many Deans are there in town? At least how many your size and shape?"

"Not many." He paused, then cleared his throat. "Not any, 'sides me. I sorta thought you might, though. Call them." He drained the last chocolate, set his cup aside, and scrambled to his feet. "Should I work on the clouds, ya think?"

We painted quietly for a few minutes before I asked, "Is there a (d)?"

"Well . . . ya might've told me t'clean it off."

"I thought of that."

He threw me a level look. "I wouldn't have."

"I think you might."

He bristled. "You couldn't make me."

"I think I could."

"No way. Not you and him t'gether." He gave his total attention to an area of dark blue. "Gramma says I'm the stubbornest person she knows."

"She doesn't know me." I stepped back, surveying the mural, pointing to another area that required dark blue for balance.

"It wouldn't've come off easy."

"Never in time for the reception."

His eyes widened. "A wedding one?"

"For us. Because we're new here."

He swallowed hard, his brush still, his eyes enormous. "If I'd've knowed, I'd've waited."

New warmth stirred under my throat. But I merely smiled and turned to mix more blue.

"But what I never *ever* expected," he said, "was what you done. How's this look?"

"Fine. Really fine."

He sighed deeply. "Wait'll they see it Sunday, though. They'll be so blasted mad—" He looked at me, uncertainty rampant in his expression. "I shoulda waited. In a way, though, I'm not sorry. I'd've missed this." He paused. "Would . . . *you* care?" There was an urgency in his voice that belied the casual way he stood, seeming almost not to listen. Still brushing paint, though on a spot already finished.

"Yes, Dean. I'd care. Very, very much."

He smiled. "'Cause this is fun."

"Just let's not make it a habit, okay?"

After calling his grandmother—at my insistence—to tell

her that he'd be home soon, Dean shared breakfast with us. Later, Arden and I stood in the annex, surveying the mural.

"It's a bit overpowering," he suggested.

"So is the whole idea. God sending His Spirit in the shape of a dove."

"Usually, it's depicted so . . . so mildly." He smiled. "But this is more appropriate. Because you're right, it was a strong concept. *Is* a strong concept, deserving better than water-color washes."

His eyes betrayed a concern that echoed my own. "I wonder what they'll say about it tomorrow?"

But as it happened, we didn't have to wait for Sunday to get the first reactions.

CHAPTER 7

By the time the breakfast dishes were washed and drying in the dish rack, every bone, tendon, and muscle in my body cried for the sleep they'd rejected the night before.

Arden said that Pam, Fritz, and he would practice his sermon, watch a few of their favorite cartoons, go for a walk and ice cream, and generally give me a chance to rest. But when I woke to post-noon sounds and sunlight, it was Lelia who was reading to Pam on the living room couch.

I felt hot with shame. Surely McClintock would frown on a minister's wife rising after noon. But I asked as casually as possible, "Did Arden show you the mural?"

"Pam and Fritz did." Her free hand described a massive arc. "I couldn't believe it!"

Claiming the far end of the couch, I laughed.

She flushed. "I meant . . . I like it . . ."

"But?" I prompted.

"I just didn't expect it."

"Neither did we—" and then I stopped. Arden and I had agreed not to broadcast details of the mural's inception. Not just yet. "We'll all get used to it, I imagine."

"I . . . hope so."

"There's something we need to discuss, Lelia. We just can't allow you to spend so much time with Pam without—"

"No!" The harsh downward movement of her hand was no less vehement than the closed look in her eyes. "No. I . . .

I come here because I want to. If you insist on paying, then I won't be able to. And that would be tragic."

Pam, picking up on the intensity in her tone, whimpered closer into the curve of Lelia's arm.

She added, less rigidly, "It's a kindness to let me come."

I stopped short of further argument. "You're the one who's been kind," I said, and held out my arms to Pam, already half asleep. "Here, Pammie. Let Mommy take you to bed."

She shrank closer to Lelia. Watching me archly from beneath the curl of her long blonde lashes, she said, "Leeya take."

I wasn't prepared for the pang beneath my ribs. Never, not even with Arden, had Pam shown preference for anyone over me. I told myself that it was natural, that Lelia was new, attentive, while my attention had been pulled in a dozen directions these past weeks; that Lelia allowed her to get away with more than I would. But the pain persisted.

And though I was sure that I'd masked it well, erasing it from my face in seconds and not allowing it to tinge my voice at all, I caught just the faintest hint of gloating in Lelia's eyes.

Dear God, I prayed as she carried Pam upstairs, what next? I'd lost the church I loved, the friends, the closeness to other people who reveled in the arts and the university. And now—to lose Pam?

"You always embroider the problem," Dr. David had said fondly, soon after I'd begun treatment. "The cold sore becomes cancer. Terminal, at that. You're not satisfied with making a mountain out of a molehill; you create a total galaxy of woes from one small meteorite!"

And he'd been right, of course.

Just because Pam preferred Lelia for tucking-in duty this one time didn't mean that she'd bypass me when choosing her wedding dress.

By the time Lelia had tiptoed down the stairway, her eyes still lit with pleasure, I'd gained perspective.

"A cup of tea?" I offered.

"I have to get home. It's another Bingo night." She turned at the doorway, her eyes darkened again. "You haven't forgotten the pepper-potatoes, have you?"

"Well, maybe last night, with my hands wrist-deep in latex, I forgot. But I'll get them started, right away."

She smiled stiffly. "I'm making nut bread. And baked beans for Grandmother." She half-opened the door and, standing there, seemed to sag. "I'm . . . sorry she wanted me to take her up."

I made my voice casual. "Don't worry about it."

"But I do. I don't want anything to keep me from coming here."

"Don't worry," I said again. "I'm glad Pam likes you."

Still, she stood there, unmoving, while three flies whizzed past her head into the kitchen.

"Did you ever think, sometimes—" Her voice clogged with tears. And with something else I recognized all too well. Quiet desperation. She cleared her throat. "Did you ever wonder if you might be . . . going crazy?"

Closing the door, I spoke gently, to rob my words of flippancy. "Better than wondering," I said, "I actually did it."

She jerked convulsively.

"I was . . . institutionalized," I said. "For several weeks." The teakettle whistled tentatively.

"But—nobody would ever guess!" She paused, dropping her voice to a near-whisper. "Does anyone here know?"

I shrugged. "Probably not." Once Dr. Connelly had found someone willing to accept a problem charge, he'd be careful not to jeopardize the appointment.

"I won't tell anyone," Lelia promised, her voice unsteady.

"Thanks. But, I'm cured. If they find out, they find out."

I drew her to the table, and she sat, woodenly, while I reached for tea mugs. "I used to question why anything so horrible should happen to me. Sometimes," I admitted, "I still do. But only when I forget the blessing."

She frowned.

"When I encounter someone who's depressed, I can share in a way no one else could—no one who hasn't also tasted the blackness."

"Blackness?" she shuddered. "Oh, yes! But . . . blessing?"

"Strange, isn't it? All our lives, we hear clichés like 'It's always darkest before the dawn.' And yet when we're closed in by that darkness, smothered by it, filled by it . . . when it seems that light, ever again, is impossible—"

"Please. Don't . . ."

I poured the boiling water over the tea bags. "There's a Bible verse that helps. Isaiah 45:3."

Accepting the tea, she wrapped her hands around the mug, as though needing its warmth.

"And I'll help in any way I can."

She nodded, seeming only to half-hear.

"Arden will talk with you, too, if you wish."

"Rev. Winters did, a few times, and it was wonderful. But one day he said he couldn't, anymore. I knew he felt as bad as I did. He wouldn't meet my eyes, and his throat was full. Poor man. Mrs. Winters had so many problems of her own—" She broke off, picking up the mug, then setting it down. "Do you mind if I ask—"

I smiled. "If I minded, I wouldn't have told you anything, would I?"

"Then . . . why you? You're educated. Talented. You have a wonderful husband and a beautiful little girl. You seem to have everything anyone could want."

"That's what I told myself when it was going on, when

God didn't seem to hear a word I was screaming to Him, and when my mother said that she didn't want to hear any more such nonsense . . . that I should just pull myself out of it and count my blessings."

"Did you ever consider . . . ?"

"Suicide?"

She nodded.

"Many times. In my mind, back then, it seemed it would have been the greatest kindness I could have done Arden and Pam. But somehow they always pulled me back—just by being there. By loving me." I shifted in my seat so that I could look at her more directly. "Anyone who says cruel things about suicides has no idea how many hells the person has suffered through before the thing is finally done. I . . . I can't say I'm glad that I went through a depression—and I'm not sure I could endure it again. But I'm not sorry it happened, either. I have so much more compassion now. So much more sensitivity. It's made me more worthy, I feel, to be a mother and a minister's wife. And a friend."

"Yes." She grasped at that. "It means a lot to me that you're my friends."

"And we are." I remembered how Arden, my artist friend Dee, and Dr. David had listened to me. How they'd tugged and jostled me back to sanity. I could never repay them for their caring—except, perhaps, by passing it on.

Lelia carried the empty mugs to the sink. "There's one more thing I'd like to ask."

"Please do."

"You mentioned the blackness—"

"Sucking me down and down. And I couldn't figure out why."

"But I *do* know why," she said wrenchingly. "I . . . was in love with someone. And he loved . . . someone else."

"I'm sorry."

"And the time before that—people got in the way. They were jealous, some of them, and others just didn't understand. Or didn't want to. Before that, there was my mother. I was never able to talk to her, and Grandmother—" she smiled fleetingly. "Well, *no*body talks to Grandmother; you just listen. I love her, though," she added, almost defensively.

"Of course. I love my mother, too. But I could never talk to her about anything sensitive and expect her to understand. And after my father died, she shut herself into a cocoon where nothing can ever touch her again. Not very realistic, and not the way I'd choose for myself. But it works for her. Her alternative to tranquilizers and psychiatrists."

"Do you think . . . do you think *I* need . . . "

I waited, but nothing more came. "No one can say that for you, Lelia. But while you're deciding, Arden and I will listen as much as you like and help however we can." I reached to touch her shoulder and could feel a slight stiffening under my fingertips. "Should I speak to him about it?"

"No!" Then, more calmly, she added, "Not yet." She smiled thinly, not meeting my glance. "I'll see you tomorrow at church."

"And at the dinner, later. Pam will want to sit by you."

When she'd gone, I wondered that I had resented her moment of triumph earlier, when Pam had preferred her. Heaven knew, there was little enough of triumph or warmth or happiness in her life.

During my morning nap, Arden had scrambled and scorched some eggs for his and Pam's lunch. I also found evidence of toast, canned peaches, and something that might once have been bacon.

The flies had settled on the peach juice, and I dispatched them with a dozen swats of a folded newspaper before washing dishes. Again.

Just as I'd marshaled enough courage to face the encrusted skillet, Dean rapped at the kitchen door.

"Can I come in?"

"Of course! It's not often I get a chance to entertain a muralist!"

He blushed. "I . . . wondered if I could see it."

"Let's leave this horrid skillet and go look at it together!"

We would have to wait in line, it seemed.

Standing on the piano bench, a young woman in faded jeans and a loose white shirt was taking an angled shot of the painting. Her camera and bulky flash attachment spoke of authority and money. Never missing a beat in her preparations, she grinned and half-waved, "I'm the press! Not *The New York Times*, I'm sorry to say, but if you want to make *The Danvers Bugle*, I'm the one who has the pull."

"*The Danvers Bugle* sounds impressive enough."

"Mrs. Templeton, right? I'm Mary Lynn Whitman, local correspondent. Births, deaths, weddings, who visits whom for a weekend, fifteen ways to serve chopped liver—you name it, I've reported it. Mostly deadly dull. That's why I keep my eye open for something unique—to spark up my copy and give me a chance for a front-page byline. This could just be it for this week."

She pulled her mouth to one side, squinted, and shot. The flash glanced across the surface of the mural.

"Now, what I think would be great is the artist and the art." Holding her camera aloft, she scrambled down from the bench. "How about right over there?" She gestured vaguely to the far side of the mural.

I smiled encouragement at Dean.

At first it seemed he might refuse. But reluctance was only momentary. He moved with a certain bravado to stand where she had indicated.

Mary Lynn turned a startled look toward me.

Dean said, "Have her, too . . . okay, Mary Lynn? She was an awful big help."

"Well, well." Mary Lynn began taking sightings again. "This *is* a story that's sure to make the front page!"

"'Specially," said Dean, "since what I was really tryin' to do was—"

"No, Dean," I cautioned.

Mary Lynn's nose was nearly twitching now. But not being a seasoned city reporter, when we'd said all we meant to, she let it go.

Good for her, I thought, and moved out of camera range, leaving Dean and his mural to star alone.

While Dean and Mary Lynn sat in a far corner getting details of the story straight, three ladies came in bearing a large roll of white paper tablecloth. We introduced ourselves, and I helped as they set up and covered more tables, stored near detachable legs in an immense closet.

Mary Lynn paused to ask when she could meet with Arden and me for an interview, and we set a time for early the following week. She threw one more admiring glance toward the mural and a quizzical one after Dean, who was disappearing down the sidewalk.

"Very interesting." She grinned reassuringly. "I used a spray can once or twice myself, in my younger, wilder days. In fact, one of my 'murals' still decorates the railroad overpass just outside East Danvers." Her expression sobered. "Dean's not a bad kid. But his mother died when he was too little to understand—if there's ever an age where a kid can accept that as anything but rejection. His dad flaked off, and that was all to the good—but a kid can't believe that. His grandmother's sweet, but she couldn't raise a flock of goldfish, let alone someone as complicated as Dean. What he's needed for a long time is for someone to take an interest in him—to see his potential." Unexpectedly, she hugged me.

"I'm glad you came! More people than Dean Kettering need someone like you around here!"

Kettering. So *that* was his last name!

The three women had been half-working, half-watching. Their eyes sparked with curiosity, but I was counting on their being well-bred enough not to pry.

And they were.

But the next arrival was a different story.

She was sixty and florid, with both the height and the bulk guaranteed to command attention. And, if those failed, there were her eyes—the color of steel, brooking no non-sense. Granting no warmth.

"What's this?" she demanded, and there was no doubt that she meant the mural. "You're the minister's wife?"

"Yes," I said. "Paula—"

She ignored my proffered hand. "Hmmmph! Didn't take you long to start educating us poor ignorant village folk, did it? I told the committee that there are artists and there are *artists*." She dismissed the mural with a sneer. "We didn't have to wait for you to come, Mrs. Templeton, to know something or two about art." She strode purposefully across the annex, the other women moving aside for her, and lifted a large framed painting that lay facedown on a table. She handled it gently, with near-reverence.

It was a paint-by-number rendition of "The Last Supper."

"My great-aunt Alice, Mrs. Templeton, painted this, stating expressly in her will that it was to be given to this church and hung precisely—*there*." She nodded curtly toward the mural. "She labored over it for weeks. Months! Every brush stroke was an act of love for her Creator." Her voice throbbed. "It's been an inspiration for literally hundreds of young people who've come here to learn of a gentle God—to learn *quietly and reverently* of His plan for humankind. It was merely waiting here, Mrs. Templeton, until the annex could be repainted, as it has been, so that it could resume its rightful place. And now I come and find this—this *abomination* screaming from the wall!" She paused for the space of a quick-drawn breath. "Well, Mrs. Templeton, what have you to say for yourself? Here it's been scant days, and you've already shown that you mean to ride roughshod over our sensibilities!"

I had waited through her diatribe, wondering when she might give me a chance to respond.

But someone beat me to it. One of the table ladies, Mrs. Bancroft, slim and humped by age and by the same arthritis that had balled the joints of her fingers, said in firm, bell-like tones that sparked a bit with hoarded malice, "I never did like that painting, Minnie Kelp. I never told you that, I guess. I didn't want to hurt your feelings."

The matriarchal voice shook a bit. "And now you do?"

"Could be I'm learning from you," she said archly, then added, "I always thought number paintings were worse than . . . box cakes. Any fool can put a box cake in a pan and have it come out perfect, but it takes creativity to make a recipe of your own, trying new things with it, folding the egg whites just so—"

"Get to the point, if you must."

"Well, a first grader can color and read numbers! I always admired Da Vinci—or was it Michelangelo? No matter. I figured it was wonderful that *somebody* painted the first 'Last Supper.' I've seen photos of it, and it is truly a marvel! But making a billion copies of it is—well, just silly, that's all. And not quite honest, if you ask me. Not to call it *art*." She nodded a brisk little exclamation point and went back to covering tables.

That night, the first of the calls came, just as we were

ready for bed. Arden picked up the bedroom extension, said "Hello" several times, then hung up slowly.

"Must have been a wrong number."

"It must have been," I said, but even under the covers, even with Arden holding me, I felt chilled.

CHAPTER 8

Dr. Connelly called the next Thursday to say that he'd be stopping by.

"The mural," I guessed, and Arden said, "I figured somebody'd call him."

Minnie Kelp, I thought. In defense of Great-aunt Alice's option on wall space.

"I won't pretend to accept such blatant usurpation, Rev. Templeton," she had said while pouring coffee at the reception dinner. "Nor am I the only one who's upset that in your very first week here you should take such liberties with a building you're being permitted to use only through the generosity of others. Perhaps, in future, you and your wife will consult with older and wiser heads than yours."

"Thank you for the coffee—Mrs. Kelp, is it?" Arden said pleasantly, "and also for helping to prove a theory of mine—that seven out of ten people totally miss the point of each week's sermon."

"I fail to see the connection!" she said crisply, but her face colored.

"So do I," I confided when Arden and I had successfully maneuvered our food to the head table. "What in your sermon had any relationship to what happened just now?"

"I don't know," he smiled. "I wasn't listening either."

I giggled. "Well, I know someone who'll be listening very closely from now on. And probably taking notes."

More seriously, he murmured, "Then remind me to preach about loving our brothers and sisters in Christ."

Other than that slight skirmish with Mrs. Kelp, Sunday had been pure pleasure.

"The honeymoon," Dora Kuhn had whispered, while members of all three churches moved in lines past long tables laden with casseroles and desserts. "Enjoy it while you can. I saw Minnie Kelp sharpening her claws—but at least she's openly malicious. Some of the others will look you straight in the eye and smile while plotting your public execution. Believe it. *Please.*" She moved on, and Skinny, lumbering behind her with two loaded plates—both his—managed only to grin his greeting.

"Nice people," Arden said. "And great food!"

It was during cleanup that Tim Linn drew me aside and whispered, "*I* sure like t'paint, Mrs. Templeton." He nodded toward the mural. "S'pose there's another wall someplace needs paintin'?"

I gave my answer enough time that he wouldn't feel rejected. "Not just now, I'm afraid. But if I hear of one, I'll let you know."

And before the afternoon was over, it seemed that such an opportunity might indeed present itself.

A shy, slender woman who'd been sitting with Dora and Skinny waited off to one side until nearly everyone had gone. "I just haven't been able to keep my eyes off the mural, Mrs. Templeton," she said, even then turned toward the painting rather than toward me.

"Paula," I insisted, almost mechanically. It had been a long day.

"Paula," she agreed, extending her slim hand. "Amy. From East Danvers, remember?" She shrugged. "But how could you yet? I'm not an artist myself, though I'd love to be a writer someday, and have often thought if I hadn't loved writing, I'd have tried to paint." She smiled, her blue eyes crinkling at the corners. "The two satisfy the same . . . soul need. Almost an itch you have to scratch."

How often Dee and I had discussed the compulsive nature of creativity! "A driving force," I agreed. "Without brakes."

"So few people understand!" She sighed, then asked, "Does your husband? Understand, I mean?"

"In a way. He's driven, too—though in a much more efficient, uncluttered way than I am."

"You're very, very lucky."

"Because I'm driven? Or because I'm cluttered?"

But she refused to smile. "Because you're understood," and there was such yearning in her voice that I stopped smiling, too, and reached to touch her arm.

"I'm sorry," I said. "I shouldn't have joked about it. But, since we've found one another, we've really got to get together and talk. I'll show you some of my paintings. And you can read me some of your work. What is it you write?"

"Poetry, mostly. Not rhymed and rhythmed," she added almost apologetically. "More . . . open. Turk says—"

My surprise at hearing the name must have registered in my eyes.

"My husband," she explained, almost without expression. "He says that poetry can't be poetry without the rhyme. Though he wouldn't read it anyway." She paused. "I guess most men hate poetry."

I couldn't answer. I was still reeling at the thought of this shy, sensitive woman sharing a life with Turk. Such a nickname was surely unique in such a small community. And the Turk we'd met would certainly hate poetry. Or music. Or beauty of any soft and gentle kind.

"I'd like to read some to you!" she was saying. "But Turk hates for me to go much of anywhere. I only go to church because it's worth the price."

"The price?"

"A few hours of silence. The cold, burning kind."

Yes, I told myself, I really am very, very lucky.

"We might be able to meet in the park," she said. "And sometimes I walk to the woods, back of town."

"I was there the other day, sketching!" I rejected the memory, the feeling, of being watched.

Her face glowed. "I love it there! But Turk—" She broke off, straightening her shoulders as though to shrug away a heaviness. "But the reason I really wanted to talk to you . . . I don't suppose you've seen the basement of East Danvers Church."

"Not yet." East Danvers was one of the three churches in the charge. That first Sunday morning we'd gone directly from there, to Peachstone, to McClintock. With the unfamiliarity of settings and formats, the flurries of greetings and introductions, and the unaccustomed fifteen-to-twenty-minute journeys between, even the sanctuaries were a blur just then, except for McClintock's.

"Well, the Sunday school rooms are in the basement, and it's really dismal. Furnace pipes overhead, painted a really hideous green, like unripe apples that have started to rot." She shuddered.

So did I. "Couldn't they paint them, at least?"

"They just did."

"Oh."

"But it's the walls that are really bad. You can avoid looking up, but there's no way to ignore those walls. They're a little . . . leprous. And very bald. I was wondering . . ." and her glance strayed to the mural again.

"I already have a volunteer to help!"

Her face glowed. "And I could get you a dozen more who'd like to have their fingers in paint!"

Paint and children, I thought. The magnet and the metal.

She promised, "I'll get back to you later this week."

"Plan to stay for tea and read me a poem or two."

Her excitement was ebbing. "I'd probably just call on the phone—"

Of course. Turk. "Then *I'll* have the tea while you read!"

She was really very pretty when she smiled. "I hope you stay for years and years and years," she said.

Thanking her, I remembered a bit uncomfortably that I'd already heard that—first from Lelia, then Mary Lynn, now her. By verbalizing the wish, they showed their fear that there was little chance of its coming true.

That night, lying on the margin of sleep, I realized that my bitterness was fading. Serving McClintock would be difficult, but challenging. And I'd already found people I could share with, just as I had in the city. Given time, if the Kelp faction would grant the time, we could grow taproots here, too. Perhaps even branches.

I'd descended through those first warm, mushy layers of sleep when the phone rang. Struggling upward, groping, I reached for the extension on the bedside table and murmured, "Hello?"

There was only silence at first. Pulsing silence.

I sighed, wanting only to plunge into sleep again. "Hello?"

And then the sound came—a low chuckling. Was it truly evil, or was it only that my mind, sleep-numbed, misinterpreted? And then the receiver clicked, and I didn't have to worry about it. I was far too weary for concern. For fear. Even for anger.

I just went back to sleep.

There was another call the next morning, but Arden took it while I made toast.

"Wrong number," he said, and poured cream into his coffee.

"Again?"

"Again?"

"Don't you remember? The other night?"

He frowned. "Maybe you got it."

"Well, I got one last night. You never heard it ring. But . . . wasn't it Saturday? You said it was a wrong number then."

He took a swallow of coffee, and his eyes clouded. "Of course I've had a lot on my mind."

Fumbling the toast, I reached for the butter knife. "What did this one say?"

"Asked for Charlie."

I handed him a slice of toast. "I thought he might have laughed."

"Well, she did when she found out I wasn't Charlie."

"I mean—instead of saying anything. The one last night did. Just laughed."

"Just . . . laughed?"

"I was pretty much asleep though." I took a bite of toast and wished for grape jelly. "Still . . ." and I shivered involuntarily.

Arden's glance, steady on me, was troubled. He chewed carefully. Contemplatively.

He was remembering the prelude to my breakdown, I knew. And I braced myself. But there hadn't been telephone calls then. And the laughter last night had really happened. Of course, with the breakdown, everything had seemed real, too—my paranoia justified.

I shuddered again.

Arden cleared his throat. "Everything's going to be okay, honey."

I became very busy with my cereal. "I know that," I said, too loudly. "Just last night I was thinking that I don't hate it here as much as I thought I would."

"Good!" His tone was warm. Relieved.

Of course, I added to myself, we've barely begun.

The Danvers Bugle, a weekly, arrived on Wednesday, the front-page story outlined with red marker, with Mary Lynn's scrawled initials decorating one corner.

The mural had photographed well, as had Dean, looking shy and proud, simultaneously. And the story was beautifully written. I read it through twice before taking the paper to Arden, who was putting the final stamp of organization on his upstairs study. While he read, I looked enviously about the tidy room. Already he'd made it home. His Bibles—several translations and versions—lay within easy reach of both his typing stand and his desk, with its clean red blotter pad, surrounded by organizers for pens, pencils, and paper. The ceiling-high metal bookshelves along one wall were lined with commentaries and reference works he'd accumulated during seminary and since. On the paneled wall opposite hung his framed diplomas, a few awards, our wedding photo, and snapshots of Pam, our families, and the city church.

I sighed, wishing that his flair for organization were contagious.

And yet Dr. David, his kindly face crinkling, his hand warm and dry on my arm, had often urged, "You've got to learn to *like* yourself, Paula. Both your strengths and what you see as weaknesses. Be honest, now. Would you trade your talent for painting to be expert at dusting furniture?"

And of course I'd had to reply that I wouldn't. Even the possibility left me feeling so desolate that I'd whispered a quick inward prayer of cancellation.

Smiling, Arden refolded the newspaper. "Even Mrs. Kelp should admit that the church got some positive coverage."

But we both knew that she wouldn't. I wondered what advice benevolent Dr. David might offer to assuage *her* insecurity and anger.

"Maybe we should get some extra copies," Arden said. "I'd like to send Dr. Connelly one."

But it wasn't necessary. For Thursday morning he called to tell us he'd be stopping by later that day.

When Dr. Connelly arrived, Arden was in the sanctuary, thinking through his sermon for the following Sunday, and Fritz watched languidly while Lelia and I, with Pam's "help," planted baby marigolds along the broken sidewalk that slanted, sometimes precipitously, toward the wooden steps and the street. Once, straightening too quickly, I experienced the familiar nausea, the unreasoning fear, that afflicted me even on stepladders—and that had made my larger murals a team effort. Arden had held the ladder, steadying the backs of my knees, and issuing periodic reassurances.

"Mrs. Winters always had petunias here." Lelia gestured broadly to include the flower beds flanking the west side of the parsonage. "And pansies on the north. But Rev. Martin talked about marigolds. He just wasn't here long enough to plant any." Her face was turned away, but there was no mistaking the heaviness in her voice. "I like marigolds. They're like little suns, glowing."

I was telling her about the year I'd seen them still blooming in November, under light snow, when Fritz roused and I heard the big car pull up. Dr. Connelly disembarked slowly.

Undaunted by the warm, late spring weather, he wore the same three-piece suit he had worn when he'd asked us to transfer to McClintock. He carried both raincoat and brief-case.

"Paula. Lovely day." There was no smile. No lilt in his voice, such as the day deserved.

"Arden's in the sanctuary!" I said, wiping a hand across my forehead and feeling the grime streak there.

He frowned. "Could you join us there, please?" As though knowing that I would—that I must?—he didn't wait for an answer, just turned toward the church.

Sighing, I wiped my hands on the grass.

"I'll finish," Lelia said. "And I'll watch Pam. You just . . . don't let him bother you."

Impulsively, I bent to kiss her cheek. Startled, she drew away, then flushed. "Don't let him send you away," she said. "Please."

I nodded, then hurried toward the kitchen door.

Halfway there, I slowed.

No. He wouldn't send us away. Not if I could help it. Not when he'd disrupted our lives to bring us here. Nor would I allow him to stampede me into worry and hurry, putting me at an immediate disadvantage. My fluster to his coolness; my grubby fingernails and muddy denim knees versus his three-piece impeccability.

Deliberately, I walked into the house, showered, brushed my hair, applied fresh makeup, and donned a crisp white blouse and flowered wraparound skirt.

Then, still slowly, I made my way to the sanctuary—not through the annex, but by the front entrance. Lelia gave me a smile of approval and a thumbs-up sign.

Dr. Connelly looked up from his conversation with Arden, and I could tell that the score was even. He had the power, but I had the calmness. Arden apparently knew it, too, for he gave me an encouraging little smile as I slipped into the pew beside him.

Dr. Connelly glanced at his watch. "Maybe we can get started now. I have to be in Ambridge by 5:30." He added, a little snappishly, "You knew I was coming, Paula."

"To see Arden, yes. And you probably remember, Dr. Connelly, that there are a million things to get in order when you're moved to a new charge."

He acknowledged that with a small "hmmmph" as he reached into his briefcase and withdrew a letter. "I realized when I received this that you, at least, Paula, had been *very* busy."

I kept myself calm. "Have you shown him the mural, Arden?"

"I insisted we wait for you," Dr. Connelly intruded. "The mural itself isn't the point anyway. Not its quality, its aesthetic value, or whatever. Rather, the fact that it was done without board approval. Without any *request* for board approval."

Able to keep the smile from my lips but not from my voice, I said, "Probably Dean didn't know he was supposed to ask for it."

"Dean? Who is Dean?"

"Didn't Mrs. Kelp mention the eleven-year-old artist?"

I had scored with her name, I could tell, but he covered quickly. "Eleven! No wonder the woman's angry! Although . . . " His tone altered subtly, and he opened the letter, reading it again, frowning, "she seemed to think that you—"

"Oh? Well, she'd know better now, since the article in the paper."

"What article?"

I sighed. "Dr. Connelly. I hope I'm not speaking out of turn, since I'm only the *wife* of the minister here. But I seem to be the one on the carpet, and I resent it."

His face flared, and his hands clenched on his knees.

"I'm not questioning your right—even your responsibility—to come here and talk over problems you see arising. But you didn't come to talk. You came ready to attack—just on the basis of that letter. And *you* were the one who told us that this charge was a trouble-spot, that it destroyed ministers, that it 'needed a good clean church fight and a split'!"

He heaved a slow, steadying sigh, then nodded. "I said that I needed a strong minister's wife here." He smiled slowly. "It seems I have one."

I returned his smile. And, suddenly, we were there to talk, to share, to explore and solve a problem rather than trying to place blame.

And I'd done it!

"You undersell yourself," Dr. David had said. "You call yourself a klutz—"

"I *am* a klutz! I bump into wastebaskets and furniture. I say the wrong thing. I do the dumbest, *dumbest* things."

"Who says they're dumb?

"Well, anyone can *tell*—"

"Because you admit to klutzhood, they accept your self-analysis. Think of yourself as a contributing, witty, worthwhile person, and they'll accept that just as readily."

"Now," said Dr. Connelly, in control again, "tell me about Dean."

After he'd heard the whole story, after he'd seen the newspaper clipping and the mural itself, we went to the house for coffee.

Lelia and Pam were in the kitchen, which was fragrant with the smell of warm coffee cake.

"Just a mix," Lelia admitted. "I borrowed it from Mrs. Campbell."

"Beautiful," I whispered. "If he hadn't already decided

that he's pleased with us, the coffee cake would have done it."

"Then . . . things are okay?"

"Better than okay!"

"He *likes* the mural?"

I smiled at the surprise in her voice. "Well, he hasn't asked me to do one on his living room wall. But he thinks we did the right thing, under the circumstances." I gathered cups and saucers, not wanting to delineate the circumstances.

But Lelia knew, as perhaps most of the people in town would know. "If you'd made him clean it off," she agreed, "he'd have been even more hostile. Now, he struts around town like he *is* somebody! Dean needed that."

This time, she offered her cheek for kissing.

CHAPTER 9

With the closing of school just two weeks away, the tempo of life in McClintock accelerated.

Two days after Dr. Connelly's visit, Madge Pears came by to talk about Vacation Bible School. Adjusting her scarf and arranging the pleats of her flowered skirt, she settled into the chair nearest the kitchen door. "It's time we get started," she said.

I nearly spilled the cup of coffee I'd poured for her. "You mean it isn't planned yet?"

"My dear. It's more than three weeks away!"

"In the city—" I broke off, but finished the thought in my mind. In the city church, they'd begun planning for the next year's Bible school before the current sessions were completed.

"Of course, city children are more uppity. Ain't they? Here, we're relaxed." She stirred cream into her coffee. "To tell the truth, we was waitin' for you and the Reverend."

"Have you mentioned this to him yet?"

"We thought you'd do crafts, since you're already into art kinds of things," she said, ignoring my question. "Don't have to be fancy. Or expensive, heaven knows! We have some feathers. Pipe cleaners. Popsicle sticks. All kinds of leftovers from other years. And we don't generally get too many out. Except for little ones, and they like t'do anything." Although she paused for breath and a sip of coffee, she kept me on hold with a wide gesture and an upraised forefinger. "Emily Sinclair does music. Has for thirty years or more, and if we *did* have someone else t'ask, we couldn't. Some of the older girls help. They've worked in a few new songs these past few years—the ones Em didn't think were modern or swingy enough t'be blasphemous."

I groaned inwardly.

"Minnie Kelp takes Intermediate, and I help Lelia in Primary. With the Reverend takin' the high school class, we'll be in fine shape." She must have caught my look of distress, for she added quickly, "The pastor *always* teaches the high school class."

"But have you *asked* him yet?"

"No need t'ask. We've always done it this way!"

"But—the other churches—"

"Can get their own teachers. They manage." She widened her eyes in alarm. "He won't mind, surely. Why, he won't even need t'plan—just talk off the top of his head—since we won't be usin' books, anyway."

"No wonder we saw so few young people here last Sunday!" Arden said at lunch, when I broke the news.

"What can you do about it?" I asked.

"Well." He was pacing beside the table, and he took three steps before answering. "One thing I'm *not* going to do is teach that class!"

I waited, tense.

"Better to skip a year than do a thrown-together Bible school. In fact," —he took three more steps— "I may suggest that they send their kids to Peachstone this year. Dan Foster told me what they're planning there. Sounds good. And it's not till August. Gives us time to hire a bus to transport—*yes!*" He stopped suddenly. "Why not a whole-charge Bible school, at least for this year? Pump all our resources into that one; then, for next year, plan something for McClintock with some worth and vitality."

Of course Dan would have to get board approval, but as education chairman . . . "East Danvers, too?"

"If they haven't planned anything. I haven't heard." Arden sighed. "I can't force McClintock to go along." He paused. "But I *can* let them know that *I* won't take a class. Not in a non-program like that."

Nor would I. I drew a deep sigh of relief. I'd always hated the feather, pipe cleaner, and Popsicle stick crafts, which often did nothing more than keep little fingers out of mischief.

"Should I call Madge? Give her some warning?"

"No. It'd be all over town in less than an hour, and all out of proportion long before morning. They wouldn't even hear what I say." He sighed. "Some won't anyway. Though, maybe I should get in touch with Dan. See if Peachstone could expand to include everyone. Would you be willing to help with crafts there, if you're needed?"

"Of course."

Nodding, he went to the phone. And I prayed for craft projects with value.

I was helping Pam corral her spaghetti when Arden finally returned to the kitchen to tell me that Dan thought Peachstone could handle McClintock's young people and East Danver's, if they wanted to join in.

Pam, delighted at seeing her daddy, flapped her spoon up and down, splashing spaghetti sauce like winter slush. One spatter hit Arden squarely on the mouth.

"Mmmmmm," he said, licking his lips. "Good!"

Giggling with delight, she bent over, her chin almost in the mess, and peered up at him. "'Gain," she begged. "Do again."

But the phone signaled another call, and he went to answer, while she returned dispiritedly to the spaghetti game.

"For you, hon!" Arden called. Despite a dread that I knew was unreasonable, I went to take the receiver. "I'll assume lunch duty," he said. "With any luck, I can give her the instant replay she craves."

The voice on the phone was light and hesitant. "This is Amy," she said. "Amy Turkle?"

So that was how Turk had earned his nickname, rather than in tribute to a swashbuckling image.

"What I called about," she said hurriedly, "is the East Danvers basement. They would like the mural. Some of the other women were at the reception last Sunday, too, and they're really excited! We thought we might involve the older kids during Bible school. The last week in June. Would that be all right with you?"

"As far as I know. We were just wondering today if you'd planned to have a Bible school this year."

"I should have told Rev. Templeton before this. We're using the new materials from the denomination—you probably know the series—on Old Testament people. We thought maybe the mural could be Old Testament, too, to carry through the theme. I just wanted to make sure you could help with it. Oh, and Dean and Tim, too—and any of the other McClintock kids."

"They'd never forgive either of us if they were excluded! And now, let's hear the poem."

She giggled nervously. "I'd be too embarrassed over the phone! And Turk's due back soon. Maybe I'll copy a few off and give them to you tomorrow. Will you be with Rev. Templeton at all three churches again?"

"I hope to every Sunday."

"Good luck! Every other pastor's wife has gotten roped into teaching Sunday school at McClintock. We hardly ever

saw Mrs. Winters. But . . . I'm sorry. I'm sure you don't need
to hear gripes from the past. I'll see you tomorrow!"

And still another involvement began that afternoon,
when Arden met with Dean, his gang, and seven other boys
at the park to talk about forming a baseball team.
Pam and I walked along with Arden to the park. Or,
rather, Arden and I walked while Pam rode in her stroller,
punishing her ancient teddy bear, who apparently hadn't
learned how to act on an outing.

McClintock was a sleepy little town at any time, by any
standards, but on a Saturday afternoon it seemed like a Mex-
ican village at siesta time. An old man sat dozing over his
newspaper on one of the benches beyond the water fountain,
not yet turned on for the nice weather. Three squirrels scam-
pered about on a large cement slab, which—Dean told us—
was where the cook tent would be set up for Firemen's Old
Home Week, early in July. Across the street, a teenage girl
dawdled along with a bag of groceries propped against her
hip, while she watched her reflection in every window she
passed.

Sleepy. Innocent. Safe. Those adjectives seemed to
describe McClintock that afternoon.

Leaving Arden and his boys to chase balls in the park,
Pam and I took the long way home, past the grocery store,
where I picked up a loaf of bread and some longhorn cheese.

"I loved Mary Lynn's write-up," Dora said as she rang me
through. "We've heard a lot of comment this week."

"Not all of it good, I'm sure."

"Most of it, though," she said comfortingly. "I know of at
least six people who're coming out to church tomorrow just
t'see it. Tell that husband of yours t'bait his sermon real
good!"

"It may already be baited."

She arched an eyebrow and pursed her lips, but didn't ask any questions.

Long before we reached the house, I saw the marigolds. Or, rather, I didn't see them, and couldn't understand why. Maneuvering Pam's stroller up the gentler slope far to the side of the stairway, I parked it beside the house, lifted her out, and went to investigate.

What on earth—?

"Oh! Posies!" Pam chirped, obviously enchanted by the tiny uprooted plants, laid in neat rows.

Like gravestones, I thought. And shuddered.

Who could have done this? It couldn't have been Fritz, who was safely in the cellar in any event. Or any animal. This was too neat. Too . . . malicious.

Malicious? Or mischief related to spray cans of paint?

No, a hostile child might have stomped the marigolds, or even ripped them out and scattered them over the street. This was . . . more threatening.

I chided myself, asking how marigolds, in any form, could translate as threat.

And yet I knew the threat was there. And the very neatness of the arrangement suggested a patience that would wait . . . and wait . . . and wait.

Dr. David, I need you.

Helplessly, I looked around. For Dr. David? For whoever had done this and might, even then, be watching for my reaction?

I forced myself to an outward calm, knowing that I could maintain the facade only through action. Through scraping small craters for the drying roots, pushing the plants firmly into place, bringing water from the kitchen, tamping the earth firmly, seeing those "little suns," as Lelia had named them, upright again.

They'd grow, I was sure. Marigolds were hardy. Far more hardy than I felt, with my inward quivering. The roots couldn't have been exposed for long. They'd live—

The telephone shrieked, and catching Pam up into my arms, I hurried into the house, only to listen to a dial tone.

Just as well. If it had been the anonymous laughter, or the marigold brutalizer . . .

It rang again.

I swallowed with difficulty, willing myself to sound confident. Capable.

"Hello. Templetons."

"Is the Reverend there?" A brusque voice I didn't recognize. Businesslike without friendliness.

"I'm expecting him soon. Could I give him a message?"

"Tell him to keep them kids off the park grass, if he knows what's good for him!"

Then the click. The dial tone.

"What next, God?" I asked aloud, and Pam looked at me strangely before returning to her play.

Next, as it turned out, came a happy surprise. A quick tapping on the door, and Amy Turkle's voice calling my name.

"You can't know how glad I am to see you!" I hugged her, and, after a moment of stiffness, perhaps surprise, she laughingly returned my hug.

I said, "Your coming makes everything right again."

"A bad afternoon?"

"Worse than bad. But nothing a cup of hot tea and a poem or two won't cure."

She followed me to the kitchen. "I feel . . . strange, reading my poetry to anyone." She hesitated.

"Maybe even vulnerable?" I supplied. "I feel that way when I show one of my paintings for the first time. We put so much of our heart's blood into our work. If someone hates it—"

"They're rejecting *us*," she said.

I set the teakettle on the burner. "I promise I'll be gentle," I smiled, and she began to read, quietly, almost expressionlessly, allowing the words to generate their own considerable power.

I'd been only dimly aware of Arden's entry. When Amy finished the fourth poem, when I found myself breathing normally again, when she looked up shyly, almost fearfully, I heard his murmured "Wow! You *wrote* those?" But his words were more a statement of awe than a question.

I moved to stand beside her, to hug her shoulders. "Amy—" My voice caught in my throat.

Folding the pages tightly, she pushed them back into her purse, and I wanted her to know how deeply they'd touched me. I'd glimpsed her soul!

"Oh, Amy," I said. "If only I could paint as beautifully with a brush as you have with words!"

Her smile was tremulous. "I've never read them to anyone before."

"But would you again?" Arden asked. "Would you read them in church?"

An expression of fright altered her eyes. "I'll . . . think about it," she said stiffly, and Arden, surely sensing her uncertainty, excused himself. Moments later, I heard his voice mingled with Pam's as they watched TV.

Wordlessly, Amy and I sipped our cooling tea. In my mind, her images, her perceptions, flowed like rapids— covering the rocky turbulence beneath the surface.

Her breathing was uneven, and when I glanced at her face, turned slightly away, I caught expressions of gratification. Of self-doubt. Of fear.

"You don't *have* to read in church, you know," I said, but she began speaking at the same time.

"I've got to go!" She stood so swiftly that her chair tumbled backward, and she barely saved it, stammering an apology as Fritz eased to safety under my chair. "I didn't realize how late it was!" She hurried toward the kitchen door, then stepped back as a heavy tread touched the back porch and Fritz yipped a tardy warning.

"Too late . . ." Subdued terror throbbed in her voice.

Turk entered without knocking. Remembering the tiny mouse under his heavy boot, I shuddered.

I glanced toward the hallway. The sound of the television would cover our voices. Unless I screamed, I thought, smiling grimly. And I had no intention of screaming.

Certainly Fritz—huddled, whining querulously— offered no help.

"Ain't you going t'offer me some tea?" asked Turk, and his mouth curved humorlessly. Standing there, he looked darkly handsome, like some rogue from centuries before.

Only by bracing myself did I hold my ground. "Of course."

He threw back his head, laughing almost soundlessly, breaking off only when he lost his balance and caught himself against the stove.

He'd been drinking.

"Well, I don't want your tea," he said. "I come for my woman." Bowing in Amy's direction, he reached out, softly caressing her cheek.

She stiffened.

"Come here, woman," he said, and she complied. But she seemed breathless. Braced. Wary.

He caught her to him, fondling her hair. "Ain't she a pretty one?"

I nodded, then added, "Talented, too."

"Talented?" His tone was mocking, and Amy's expression was so pained that I chastised myself for having spoken. "How's that?"

He hated poetry, she'd said. I tried to promise her with my eyes that I wouldn't give her away. "She's compassionate. Perceptive. All the things that count."

He nuzzled her a bit more roughly. "Well, now," he said, chuckling, "I guess that depends—don't it?—on who's counting?"

"Turk. Please—" but he hushed her with a look and continued.

"I always figured a woman's talents in the kitchen and the bedroom was what mattered." His eyes were bold on me. "Of course, your husband, bein' a minister—"

"Turk!" Amy's face flamed.

"Bein' a minister," he went on, a bit more loudly, "he don't know about the bedroom."

"There *is* Pam!" Even as I spoke, I was ashamed of having descended to his level.

Triumph glittered in his eyes. "I thought she might've come in a kit."

Amy moaned.

His eyes raked me again. "But I did think that'd be one stupid waste of good equipment."

Amy was sagging now, totally diminished. And it was only my anger at his treatment of her that kept me from feeling destroyed as well.

The sounds of the television seemed obscenely light-hearted as they covered our silence.

"Well, now," he said, his glance still on me, "I'd better take my woman home. You can see how anxious she is to get me alone."

The door had closed behind them and I'd managed to still my trembling by clutching the rim of the sink, when

Arden, holding Pam, came out and asked pleasantly, "Did Amy leave, honey?"

Rattling pans as though in preparation for the evening meal, I only nodded. I couldn't turn or speak, not while the fury still held me.

CHAPTER 10

That evening, as though vacation Bible schools and base-ball, uprooted marigolds and an encounter with Turk weren't quite enough, a young couple stopped by to ask if Arden would marry them.

"This is Angie," the boy said, almost paternally. "Angie Kleigh. And I'm Ted Fenwick."

He was just a little taller than the girl, but with such broad shoulders, compared to her slenderness, that she was reduced to fragility—a condition intensified by her pallor and the dullness in her eyes.

Not exactly a blushing bride, I thought as I picked up my book and started to excuse myself.

"Please." She reached toward me. "Please don't go."

Putting his arm around her waist, the young man drew her close. "Angie's afraid," he said, "but we both know this is what we've gotta do. We need your help, Rev. Templeton. You see . . . " Long, dark, curling lashes obscured his eyes. "I . . . got her pregnant."

"It wasn't his fault any more than mine."

"Yes, it was," he said gruffly.

"Let's talk about it," Arden suggested. "Why don't you sit down—there, on the couch."

Pam pedaled over on her tricycle to offer the girl her battered clown. Angie accepted it, her eyes gaining warmth and luster.

"It's going to be so beautiful, having our own baby. We tried to tell them that—Ted's parents and my mom—but they wouldn't listen. Just because they're sorry they had kids." She sighed. "That isn't fair, I guess. My mom's had to raise us alone for the last ten years. And Ted's mom has MS. I guess they're really worried about us. Only it comes out like anger."

Ted laid his arm across her shoulder in a singularly sweet token of pride and ownership. "Angie thinks deep," he said. "You should hear her in school. She's always got straight A's."

Angie smiled, and color touched her cheeks. "But Ted's on the football team," she said just as proudly.

For a moment, Arden and I might as well not have been in the room. I found myself wondering if Amy and Turk had ever been so gently in love. The answer came readily. Amy—of course. Turk—never. Catching Arden's glance, I saw that he was as touched as I. But we both knew the survival rate for teenage marriages. And with a baby on the way. . . .

"So we want to get married." Ted had returned his attention to us. "Both my parents and Angie's mom say it's got to be an abortion. But this is our baby they're plannin' to kill—" His voice broke, and his hand tightened convulsively on Angie's. "And we've got to protect it. Don't we?"

"How old are you?" Arden asked.

"I'm almost eighteen. And Angie's . . . " He glared at Arden. "Angie's sixteen. I was gonna lie. We'd talked about it, but . . . I guess there's nothing you can do, then, huh?"

Arden said gently, "Well, I can't marry you tonight, if that's what you mean. But there are directions we can go."

"We've tried talking to our parents!" Angie sighed.

"But I haven't. Would you mind?"

Ted frowned. "You think it might help?"

"It might. I don't know your parents. But Angie feels they love you. I imagine things are pretty hot just now."

They nodded.

"You quarreled with them today?"

"This afternoon. We told them about the baby."

"Then you've got to give them time to work through this. To process it. Filter it through their feelings for you and for themselves. Just try to see it from their point of view for a little."

They shifted uncomfortably, but Arden didn't pause. "You gave them some fairly tough news today. They've got to feel angry, betrayed—and worried. All their plans for you are in shambles."

Ted said miserably, "Angie's mom always wanted her to go to college."

"And now that dream's destroyed—at least for now. And you, Ted. You're suddenly the enemy."

Ted nodded. "All I know is, I'm gonna marry Angie. We're gonna have this baby. I . . . guess we know now it won't be easy. But we love each other, and that's what counts. Right?"

Arden smiled. "Just be prepared for those moments when you doubt your love. When you feel trapped. After I talk with your parents, I'd like to spend some time with you. We call it premarital counseling. Maybe I can help you prepare for some of those rough spots."

"Yeah." Ted looked to Angie for confirmation.

Smiling, she returned the clown to Pam. "Thanks, Rev. Templeton. You've really helped." She smiled to include me. "You, too, ma'am."

"Most of it you figured out yourselves," Arden said as he got up to see them to the door.

"Yeah," Ted said wonderingly. "I guess we did, didn't we?"

That night, when the phone rang—while Arden was in the bathroom—I was too tired to play games.

First the silence. Then the beginning laughter.

"Why don't you go back to the Fun House where you belong?" I snapped, and thumped the receiver into the cradle.

Arden appeared with a gigantic towel draped toga-like about him. Only his striped socks spoiled the image. "What was that all about?"

"Our friendly neighborhood obscene caller," I said. "I just didn't have the energy to spare tonight."

Sitting on the edge of the bed, he drew his socks off slowly. "He said something obscene?"

"Just laughed, again," I said. "But forget it. I plan to." Which might not be strictly true, I knew, once the lights were out and I waited for the phone to ring again. In a way, *wanting* it to ring—though if Arden were to answer, would the caller laugh?

Arden looked worried as he got ready for bed, and I wondered, as I forced myself to yawn and roll over, if it was because the calls were beginning to concern him, or if he still doubted my perceptions.

I was glad that I hadn't told him about the marigolds. Or about the incident with Turk.

Even before Arden approached the pulpit on our second Sunday in McClintock, I knew that the honeymoon Dora had referred to was over. At least for that third of our charge.

At East Danvers, everything had seemed fine that morning. There'd been an air of excitement about the mural, and Amy had given me copies of the Bible school workbooks for each grade level so that I could better plan the crafts.

As we drove to Peachstone, Arden asked, "Did she mention how she'd hurt herself?"

Riffling through the pages of the Primary workbook, I asked, "Who?"

"Amy."

My hands tightened, crumpling a page. *"Amy?"*

He looked at me questioningly. "The bruise on her cheek. Didn't you notice? And she seemed to be limping slightly."

Closing my eyes, I leaned back in the seat, remembering Turk's behavior of the night before. And Amy's tension. *Oh, God,* I moaned inwardly, but my anguish couldn't shape itself to further prayer.

At Peachstone, except that Dan Foster drew Arden to one side for a short, intense conversation while the choir filed in, everything went smoothly. Later, on the way to McClintock, Arden said that Dan had contacted the other Bible school planners, and all had agreed that McClintock was welcome, but they'd have to share expenses.

"They should snap at it," I said. But I knew they wouldn't.

As we drew closer to town, both of us seemed to be bracing ourselves emotionally for McClintock. Was this the way it had happened for our predecessors, I wondered. Had they mentally girded themselves for battle, knowing that it had to come? And yet I remembered reading that when nations prepared defense against war, they created the best possible climate for conflict.

Help Arden to say it well, God, I prayed, and reminded Him that He was the one who'd sent us here.

I wondered if He was getting tired of hearing that.

A couple of last-minute smokers lingered outside the church until Arden had parked, and a few latecomers hurried to get inside, just in time.

"Look, Arden!" I said. Angie and Ted waved as they mounted the steps, his arm behind her waist.

Dora Kuhn, without Skinny, waited just inside the door

for me. "No choir today," she explained, then murmured, as Arden shrugged into his robe and stole, "Thought I'd better warn you. Minnie has a real bee in her bonnet. She's been buzzing around since she got here, before Sunday school—and there's more to the hive than her."

Arden threw me a reassuring look and strode on ahead, behind the men's quartet.

"Any idea what it's all about?" Dora asked as we found aisle seats, close to the back.

"Probably so." And I smiled so that my non-answer wouldn't seem abrupt.

"No matter," she whispered under cover of rustling bulletins as the prelude died. "I love suspense."

It was during the church announcements that Arden mentioned the summer Bible school, explaining that since nothing had really been planned, as yet, for McClintock, and since Peachstone had a fine program well in hand, it was his thinking that for this year the two churches should combine their forces and their finances, creating a learning and sharing experience for children of both congregations.

There were spots of whispering, but, it seemed, no one would interrupt the service. I sent up a small prayer of thanks. Dora looked disappointed.

After a suitable pause, Arden opened his Bible, saying, "I'll welcome your comments and suggestions directly following the service."

"I'm sorry, *Mr.* Templeton, but since I won't be here after the service, I'll give you my comments and suggestions right now." It was—predictably—Minnie Kelp, standing in her pew, her body rigid and her voice like ice crystals. "I'll be leaving as soon as I've had my say here. And I doubt that I'll leave alone."

Here we go, God, I thought. *Are You going with us?*

Dora's hand clamped over my arm, as much from the excitement of the moment, I suspected, as in support.

Minnie Kelp had moved to the center aisle and was approaching the altar as she spoke. "Last week, Mr. Templeton," she said, her voice clearly for a broader audience, "we were all shocked and chagrined to find that your wife had encouraged an urchin to deface a whole wall of the annex. This week, we find that you have undermined our plans for our own Bible school."

"What plans?" Arden asked quietly. "As of yesterday, apparently, no plans had been made. No materials ordered. No course of study even chosen."

Dora drew a sharp little gasp of pleasure. Inwardly, I moaned. And mourned. This type of controversy had no place in the house of God.

"Mrs. Kelp, couldn't we discuss this after the—"

"No! You have challenged me, and I am prepared to answer. Our course of study," she continued dramatically, mounting the three steps and lifting the massive Bible from the lectern, "is the very Word of God! Would you prefer another source, Mr. Templeton?"

"Certainly not. Rather, I'd like you to let us know—all of us—those portions of the Word of God you plan to study during Bible school week. It was just a week you were thinking of, wasn't it? Half-days? A total of—oh, about three hours a day, with half an hour off for refreshments, at least that much for crafts, and another half-hour for outdoor games? Surely you weren't planning to cover the *whole Bible* in the, let's see, total of . . . seven and one-half hours, were you?"

Dora wasn't the only one who laughed at that. But that his temporary triumph would be expensive in the long run was evident in the anger that flared from Minnie Kelp's eyes. Her loss of stature could not go unavenged.

"By what authority do you patronize me, mister?"

"I answer you only because you've chosen to make this church an arena, and I do that by the authority of the One we both worship and love. Now, please, if you've had enough of this combat, as I have had more than enough—" He had obviously lowered his voice, speaking only to her, but the church, vacuum-still, guaranteed that his words reach all ears. And I was hopeful that, in the minds of rational hearers, he'd regained points lost by his levity.

I winced at my own mental terminology. This should never have been a place of combat or of competition.

But Mrs. Kelp had interrupted his plea for peace. "Never!" she said. "Never will I be conciliated, or mealy-mouthed, or subjugated in my own church! I owe you no explanation, mister. And I step down for no one!"

"Then I do step down." Firmly, Arden closed his Bible, folded his notes, and descended the three steps. "I invite all of you who will to join me in the annex to share in the remainder of the service." Although his tone was calm and his expression pleasant as his glance touched here and there about the congregation, I knew that his emotions had been jarred. How often I'd envied his ability to face any situation with an expression of calm confidence.

Dora and I joined him as he paused at our pew. Together, we entered the annex. Others moved behind us. How many, I couldn't tell, and Arden's hand on my elbow bolstered my own unwillingness to look around. Even when he'd reached the small lectern near the mural, he didn't look up, just adjusted his Bible and notes while the organist seated herself at the piano and the rest of us found seats in the front rows.

How well the mural's forceful lines and colors suited the turmoil of the past few minutes.

"Let us join together," Arden said quietly, "in hymn 273."

"I believe," Arden said, when we'd reached the parsonage, "that about two-thirds came with us."

"And some left. Embarrassed, I suppose, or disenchanted." I sighed. "Angie and Ted left."

"Too bad. Too bad."

"And those who remained in the sanctuary. What will they do next?"

"Call the district superintendent again. And maybe the bishop. We're in for some rough sledding, honey—sooner than I'd ever have thought. Are you okay?"

I reached to run my fingers through his auburn hair. "Better than okay! Proud of you."

He drew a sharp breath. "I'm not proud of myself. There must have been better ways to handle it."

The phone was never quiet that afternoon, our living room never empty.

Angers, frustrations, slights we'd been spared before were dumped into our laps, in spite of our wish not to hear them and our desire not to take sides, not to know how varied the complaints were. How deep the splits. How cherished the wounds.

"How they abused poor Rev. Winters, threatening to put his poor sick wife onto the sidewalk, bed and all."

"And her sobbing, fit to break a heart . . . "

"And that young Rev. Martin. I ask you, now, be honest. What right does anyone have to read someone else's love letters? And times are different, ain't they—looser now? Young folks come out and say what they mean, frank and honest."

"And long before that, remember how—"

"Remember when—"

"Remember who—"

"When we fight, we all lose," Arden said, over and over,

to different callers, different groups. "I plan to see Mrs. Kelp tomorrow—"

"*Not* to apologize! *She* should apologize!" many said, in one form or another.

"I'm not worried about apologies, either way. I don't believe that God is either. I think He wants to see us, not on opposing sides, but all on His side. And that's what I hope to tell Mrs. Kelp."

"You might as well bark up a bee tree! She'll never listen. All Minnie Kelp has heard for years has been the sound of her own voice."

By mid-afternoon I was exhausted, with black shadows creeping over my soul. The time, Dr. David had said, to find a place to regroup.

But I couldn't go far from the house, since, with each influx of visitors, coffee must be offered. So a walk to the woods was out of the question.

Upstairs, Lelia was reading to Pam and Fritz, and their voices rose in excitement when the story gained impetus. The annex door stood open, with people stopping by to see the mural.

So there was only the church.

I entered quietly, from the annex, my footsteps muffled by the deep-pile carpet.

It was a beautiful sanctuary. Vivid afternoon sunlight, throbbing through the stained-glass panels, enriched everything it touched. Such a place should never be a place of anger. Everything about it urged worship, peace.

Quietly, I slipped into a back pew. Without even planning it, I closed my eyes in prayer, letting the peace of the place, its intrinsic sense of worship, seep into my soul, dispelling blackness. I must have sat thus for several minutes—not really praying yet, merely preparing my soul with quietness—before I heard the quiet, desperate sound of sobbing.

Whoever it was knew deep trouble—trouble I, perhaps better than most people, could understand. Easing from the pew, I moved forward.

She was kneeling at the altar, her face in her hands, her shoulders shaking.

"Mrs. Kelp," I said, suppressing surprise. "Minnie. Please don't."

Leaning toward me, into the arm I placed about her shoulder, she breathed in long, quivering breaths that spoke of extended weeping.

And then she realized who I was and pulled away, her face contorted.

"You! How dare you touch me!" she spat. Energized by anger, she staggered to her feet. "How dare you—either of you—diminish me in the eyes of people I've known all my life!"

There was no point in trying to speak through her hatred. Indeed, I found myself shaken by the very force of it.

Her voice softened, deepened. "But I'll repay you—I promise it!—if I have to spend my dying breath to do it!"

CHAPTER 11

T hat night, I expected a phone call, but none came.

Neither did sleep—for hours. Once, when its warm mists gathered, they were dispelled by memory of Minnie Kelp's desperate weeping.

Minnie.

Yet as swiftly as pity invaded my thoughts, as I breathed a quick prayer for ease of her spirit, I remembered what she was doing to us, and softness congealed.

And she hardened her heart, like Pharaoh, I thought half-whimsically.

"Permit yourself to be human," Dr. David had said. "Allow yourself anger. Indulge in some good healthy hatred."

But Jesus required something quite different.

That settled, I again invited the mists of sleep, but still remained sharply awake, aware of each creak of settling wood, each scurry of squirrel or chipmunk along the shingles, alert to occasional cars passing somewhere a street or so away, and of something else, indefinable, near the house.

More squirrels?

Or someone uprooting marigolds?

Gently, careful not to waken him, I eased nearer to Arden, who grunted and flopped his arm across me. All too keenly aware of how much I'd miss him the next three days, the next two nights, while he attended a compulsory ministerial retreat with the district superintendent, I fought the impulse to hold him so tightly he couldn't escape. What could Dr. Connelly possibly say that would be more important than my need for him?

"Ask Lelia to stay over," he had suggested as we'd prepared for bed. "She'd love to."

"And Pam'd love to have her."

"But?"

"But I'm not a child. And I'm not . . . sick, any longer."

"I know that." He traced my eyebrow and nose with his forefinger. "I just thought, in case any more kids break in— or there are more phone calls—"

"I'll be fine. I need to be able to handle things. I guess I'd really love to do it the easy way. But I don't want to."

"That makes sense." He smiled. "But if you need Lelia, don't be—"

"Childish?" I prompted. "I won't. But if I need anybody, I'll call *you*. And you'll come charging on your sturdy steed to rescue me from whatever dragon threatens."

"Ah, yes! Only two small flaws with that myth, my dear. Our ancient Chevy moves more like a hiccuping kangaroo than a steed, and . . ."

"And?"

He sighed. "And you won't be able to reach me. The lodges are semi-primitive. But I'll call you from the conference building each evening. Fair enough?"

"Fair enough." But it was all I could do to hold my trembling until he'd kissed me goodnight and turned away, slipping into an easy, snoring slumber.

I woke next morning in a half-empty bed. Prelude, I thought, to the next two mornings. Sunlight careened through our thin curtains, which billowed in the breeze flowing between the partially opened casement and the open bedroom door. From its nest in the gingerbread, a robin sang as though it could burst.

The bed, still warm where Arden had lain, demanded another few moments of rest.

I closed my eyes, tuned out the robin, and picked up sounds from downstairs. Diluted sounds. A radio newscast, interspersed with musical advertisements, and voices. Pam must be up, too.

I stretched, stealing one last moment, slipped on my bathrobe, and padded down the stairs in my bare feet.

Oops. I braked halfway down.

Another voice. Not Pam's. Arden's and . . . whose?

No use. I couldn't distinguish it. The cadences of voices rose and fell, mingling with the weather report, the thumping of Fritz's tail on the still-uncarpeted living room floor, and the stubborn snarl of Mrs. Campbell's lawn mower.

I eased back to the bedroom and dressed.

Madge Pears was leaving as I entered the kitchen. In her crisp print, complete with jewelry, she might have been up for hours.

"Paula," she said, "I was just tellin' the Reverend here that poor Angie Blake was took t'the hospital last night."

"Angie?" I threw Arden a startled look, but his expression was calm. Naturally.

"Poor thing twisted her ankle, going down steps with a basket of laundry." She gestured broadly. "Works her like a pack mule, that mother of hers does. Though to be fair, Jane's no slouch neither."

A twisted ankle. Could she have jolted the baby? "How long—?"

"Just a day or so. They want to be sure nothin's broke. But knowin' the Reverend was leavin' this morning, and seein's that her and Ted showed up at church, I thought I'd best let him know."

"And I'm glad you did," Arden said.

"Won't you have some coffee, Madge?"

"I had breakfast hours ago!" She gave me a knowing look. "Though I guess with all the excitement here, and so many comin' and goin' yesterday, you wouldn't have got t'bed till late."

"Still," I said, not feeling the least apologetic, "I think I'd have stayed in bed. There's something marvelous about listening to a robin concerto while perfectly relaxed."

"Well, I have better things to do than listen to robins, whatever it is they're doin'. This is the week that Dianna's ex-lawyer gets his comeuppance, and I wouldn't miss it for the world."

I fished through my memory. Dianna . . . who was Dianna?

Of course! Her soap opera—"The Flame and the Fury!" Monday morning, for past generations the signal for laundry flapping in the wind, now merely meant that Madge could begin another five glorious days of immersion in fictional problems.

"It was just last week Dianna found out he was really hired by her murdered husband's first wife's daughter, who'd *love* to get her hands on Dianna's money!" She sighed, shaking her head with what passed for sadness, though her voice rang with contented excitement. "One does wonder if there's any good in the world at all these days!"

After she was gone, I asked Arden if she'd mentioned Bible school.

"Only that she knew things were safe in my hands." His eyes twinkled. "Me being a 'man of the cloth,' after all—not to mention 'looking for all the world like Jeremy.'"

"Jeremy?"

"Dianna's intended fifth husband. He's the soul of honor. An English lord, I believe, but determined to make his own way in the world by raising muskmelons and cockatoos."

"The most startling thing!" I told Arden later after he'd

shut off the engine of the car, which he'd pulled behind the house for a quick cleaning. "I didn't touch them. I wanted you to see what you think could have done it."

He threw me his slow, patient smile.

"The marigolds," I said, not nearly so patient. "When I went out to find Fritz, there they were—uprooted." I nearly added "again" but caught myself in time.

He eased out of the car. "Did you find Fritz? He's probably your villain."

"They were laid carefully in a row." I shivered, but led the way eagerly, not admitting even to myself my reasons for not having replanted the marigolds this time—for wanting him to see for himself. "There. You—" But the marigolds no longer lay uprooted. Instead, they looked healthy and contented, if a little waterlogged.

Pam called, "Me watered posies!" and waved a little watering pail to prove it.

Lelia smiled. "They really didn't need water that badly, but she insisted." She studied the plants a bit ruefully. "I hope we didn't drown them." Then she paused, studying me intently. "I hope you don't mind."

Arden cleared his throat. "I'd better get my things. Paula—could you help me?"

"No. Wait . . ."

"Something's wrong?" Lelia's voice was dull.

Pam, giggling, sprinkled the last of her water on Fritz.

Arden, with obvious unwillingness, waited.

"When you first saw the marigolds today . . . what were they like?" I finished weakly.

"Just like this. Only not quite so drowned. I hope—"

"It doesn't matter," I interrupted. "All that matters is, were they uprooted?"

She frowned. "Should they have been?"

"No, of course they *shouldn't* have been. But—"

"Paula," Arden repeated gently.

Lelia's face was a study in misery.

"It's all right," I assured her. Feet dragging like those of a child about to be set in a corner, I followed Arden, past the car, over broken sidewalk, up three steps to the creaking porch. How I wished I'd never mentioned the marigolds! My mind spun past similar memories. *"But, Arden—honey, honest, I did leave your sermon notes on the desk. I can't explain how they got in the refrigerator. All I know is that I didn't put them there. I'd remember a thing like that, wouldn't I? Anybody would! Unless she was crazy or something."* And then, as depression had deepened. *"Oh, Arden, please, please, please believe me. I saw it. I really, really did. It was right outside the window, and it was horrible, horrible."*

We'd reached the bedroom. Enclosing me in his arms, Arden said gently, "Don't worry about it."

If he'd accused me of slipping again, I could have—would have—defended myself. After all, it was simple enough. Someone had been ashamed. Had replanted the marigolds. Lelia hadn't noticed, and once Pam had literally drowned them, no one could tell the difference.

But his gentleness always undid me, made me feel so cherished that I couldn't be defensive.

"I wish I didn't have to go," he said.

I did see them, Arden, I blubbered in my thoughts. *I did!*

"Honey . . . are you sure you don't want Lelia to stay with you tonight?"

Stiffening, I pulled as far back as his arms would allow. "Yes, I'm sure," I snapped. "I *told* you I was sure!"

He overlooked that. Just held and patted me until I'd relaxed again. Then, sighing, he kissed and released me. "I'm going to be late."

"You will call tonight?"

"I will call tonight."

CHAPTER 12

Even as I watched Arden back out of the driveway and head down the street, I yearned for his call that evening.

I comforted myself with his promise while the morning dragged through housekeeping chores, while I argued Pam away from the TV to her lunch and a nap, while I worked quietly in the kitchen, not wanting to waken her.

I forced myself to write a note to Dee, asking about her pottery and whether there'd been any good art/craft shows lately, then tore it up because it sounded so lifeless. So homesick. I tried to read, but couldn't concentrate. I tossed the book aside and went to stand before my painting—willing myself into those shadows, that light, that comfort. Turning away, I walked to the annex, into the sanctuary, trying to find peace there. But restlessness, discontent, loneliness, and a vague disquietude persisted.

This is ridiculous, I told myself. Shape up! You tell Arden you're not a child, and you're no longer sick, and then you act as though you're both.

Yet I continued to pace, to fret, to check the clock, to grumble at Fritz's obvious puzzled concern, to listen for Pam's wakening sounds, to sigh, and to repeat the pattern. Even the sunshine, flooding the tracery of leaves beyond the kitchen window, and the bird-songs, exulting in the day, I found oppressive.

Setting up my easel, I squirted yellow ochre on my

palette. And stared at blank canvas for half an hour, waiting for inspiration to stir.

But at least the effort hadn't been a total waste. At least I was one half-hour closer to Arden's call.

Stupid! I scolded myself. Aren't you a person anymore? Are you just a shadow of Arden? Can't your heart pump blood or your lungs expand without his consent and encouragement?

It was when I caught myself pacing, again, and hitting a fist into an open palm, that I recognized—all too sharply—the behavior that had characterized the beginnings of my depression.

Well, it had to stop, that was all there was to it! I wouldn't go through that again.

And I wouldn't scuttle off to some other haven, now that Arden was gone, to ask for sympathy and strength.

Not that McClintock offered that many havens.

Mrs. Campbell, next door, was a scarcely ever glimpsed presence I associated with lawn mower sounds on the far side of her house.

Madge, even if she had become the good friend she was determined to be, would have been no help at all in real-life drama. Amy, who might one day be the kind of friend Dee had been, wasn't yet. And I'd hate to afflict Lelia with a tangible parallel of what she herself suffered. Especially when I had offered myself, and she had accepted me, as an example of what lies on the far, sunny side of depression.

If we'd still been in the city, I'd have called Dee.

Well, why not?

With trembling hands, I dialed her number.

I nearly gave up on the sixth ring. But then, remembering that she often had her hands in clay at her worktable in the basement and that her phone was upstairs in the kitchen, I allowed it five more rings. Breathless, she answered on the eleventh, and I smiled, picturing her with one hand half-wiped down the side of her smock, the other dripping mud, unnoticed, to the black and white kitchen tile.

"How are you?" I recognized a second symptom as emotion clogged my throat.

"Fine," she said tentatively. "Now let me ask you a question. *Who* are *you*?"

"How soon they forget," I said, laughing. Relaxing at last. "Mere weeks ago we were setting up for the show at the mall and you were telling me you'd miss me hourly, at least, and—"

"Paula?" My name came out in a yip. "Paula *Templeton*? You're calling from—that little place they exiled you to?"

"McClintock." Then, laughing, "They *have* strung the phone lines this far, you know."

"Oh, yes, I suppose so." I could almost see her shrugging. "But isn't it deadly?"

"There are moments when it's dull, yes."

"When are you getting into the city again?"

"Look, Dee, why don't you come here? Could you get away?"

There was expansive silence, but I knew that she'd be thinking it over, in all its levels—frowning—her muddy hand still dripping.

"You could come for a weekend—a whole week, if you like! We could plan an art show! The park would be perfect!" If we were allowed to trample the grass, I amended. "And there must be people around who'd love to be involved."

More silence. Then, "I suppose I could get away, for a few days at least. Not this weekend, but the one after. Would you have room for me?"

"Lots. Oh, I'm so glad you're coming!"

Another thoughtful pause stretched.

"Paula."

"Yes?"

"Why did that sound—just now—more like panic than excitement?"

I swallowed noisily. She had always been much too good at reading my moods.

She asked gently, "Troubles?"

"Nothing we can't handle. It's just—well, Arden's away for a couple of days, and I . . . I can't seem to get geared to anything. The pacing thing . . ."

"I'll be there . . . by early evening."

"No!" I said it too quickly, so I backed off and tried again. "No." There, that was better. "I'm being silly. As soon as Pam wakes from her nap, we're going for a long, long walk through the woods, and I'll feel better."

"You're sure?"

"Yes, really. Even over the phone, you have the old, soothing magic. Thanks for being there."

"If you change your mind, I'll be here all day, working."

I forced my voice to lightness. "The Whitaker show's next week!" I'd signed up for that one. A wave of the old bitterness swept over me, but I rejected it. "I hope it's fantastic!"

"Oh, it's just another show. And remember, if you need me—call."

"Hey, look. I didn't mean to worry you."

"You haven't."

But I had. All day long, working at her wheel, she would keep her ear tuned to the phone, afraid that she'd miss my panic call. "Just hearing a voice from the past was all I needed," I said firmly. "Just hearing *any* voice, really! But Pam'll be waking, and we'll take that walk. In a way, I'm sorry I called. Not sorry to talk with you! Just sorry that I communicated—whatever I communicated."

"Desperation," she said quietly, still not convinced, I knew.

"Either we have a bad connection, or you need your hearing aid adjusted," I joked.

She laughed. "Then you really are all right?"

"I really am! Get back to that wheel. And make me another of those jugs, will you? And a couple of bowls, if you have the time before you come. This place just cries for enrichment with fine pottery!"

"Just remember—no special deals for impoverished ministers!"

"But leave the price tags on, okay? McClintock might not recognize the unique qualities of your craftsmanship! They might just think I bought seconds at the discount store."

Her laughter rang over the wire in a hearty peal. "Vandal! You really are all right, aren't you?"

And I kept her convinced until we hung up.

Knowing that if Fritz went with us on our walk my entire energy would be devoted to the preservation of wildlife, I locked him in the basement.

To give the outing a picnic atmosphere, I packed some bananas and filled cakes, which Pam begged to eat even before we'd passed the senior citizen housing.

At her insistence, she carried the cakes, almost crushing them against her chest. I carried the bananas, my sketchbook and pastels.

The call had helped. And if it had revitalized my bitterness at having been shunted to McClintock, maybe that was helpful, too. In the busyness of the past weeks, in their tensions and frustrations and concerns, perhaps I'd sublimated my own feelings too much, allowing the symptoms to surface when I'd been faced with Arden's absence.

"Express your anger," Dr. David had urged. "Break a pencil, kick a tree. Give it specific verbal expression, too. Say, 'Arden, I simply can't stand the way you crumple the gum wrapper for minutes before you throw it away.' Or talk to yourself. Out loud. 'I'm angry today because it simply isn't fair that people keep breaking into line at the grocery store. Of course they're in a hurry. But so am I. Of course they have important things to do! So do I. The next time anyone does it without being invited, I'm simply going to tell them just how I feel. Calmly. Quietly. Lucidly. I'm not going to *think* it. I'm going to *say* it.'"

Perhaps, of all the strands of my treatment, this had been the most difficult to follow. I'd never before been encouraged to express anger openly. Never allowed myself to believe that I had a right to be angry.

"Everyone has a right to anger," Dr. David had insisted. "No one needs to be a doormat."

"But a minister's wife—"

"Ah, so minister's wives have to take a Doormat Vow? I reject that! Even a good tool deserves respect. How much more a person, no matter how he or she sees the role as service. I'm warning you, Paula. You've got to do it, let it out, air it. Otherwise, it's going to eat through your emotions like acid."

Dear Dr. David.

I'd really have to write and tell him how well I was doing.

It was a gorgeous day.

Pam, still a bit wide-eyed and stumbling from her nap, padded close by, in need of an occasional hand as the terrain roughened.

Even juggling Pam, bananas, and my sketching materials, I was free to indulge my senses in the touch of rough grass against my ankles, the gentle giving of moss beneath my sneakers, the snap of a twig, the roundness of a pebble, the stroke of the breeze, and the soft nudging of foliage as I bent to enter the woods near an aging oak, where the useless wire fence ended in tangle.

Bird-songs—sleepier as the afternoon lengthened, as the heat intensified—were at once a pleasant accompaniment to our walk and a numbing drug in my mind. Almost, I could sit down and go to sleep.

I shook myself against it. I wanted to exercise, to work, to tire myself so thoroughly that sleep that night, when it mattered, would not have to be courted. After Arden's call, of course.

"Bood!" cooed Pam. "Mommy see bood?"

"Yes, honey!" I held her still and watched her small finger continuing to point, even following the cardinal into an upward sweep to a higher limb.

Suddenly she crumpled, folding into a tired position on the ground.

"It's wet there, Pammie." Leaning my materials against a tree trunk, I lifted her to a dry stone and wished that I'd brought something for both of us to sit on. A small blanket. Even a bath towel.

She seemed comfortable enough, though, and content. Still hugging the cakes. Finding a place to sit, I looked about for something to sketch.

Pam, of course.

I worked quickly, afraid that she'd regain energy and explode into new explorations before I'd captured her lines.

But she didn't, and twenty minutes later I had a sketch that caught her, her happy tiredness, and the setting of leaf and shadow, sunshine, moss and sun-dappled rock.

Arden would love it. We'd frame it for his office.

It was turning out to be not such a bad day after all!

"Want to go for another walk?" I asked, and Pam nodded sleepily, scrambled to her feet, and held up her arms to be carried.

Well, why not? I wanted to be tired. I closed the cover of the drawing pad over the sketch and weighted it with a small stone at each corner. Then, picking up the bananas, cakes, and Pam, I set off deeper into the woods.

Walking along, savoring, remembering, I thought just once of the first time I'd walked there. Of the eerie sensation of being watched.

Uncannily, it came again.

"Mommy needs to rest, honey." I set Pam down, arched my shoulders, rubbed my lower back, and, as casually as possible, turned slowly, studying the entire circumference of wooded area.

And my eyes caught movement, just at the edge of vision.

I stiffened, watching, until Pam decided that enough was enough and tugged at my shirttail.

I'd seen nothing else, and the earlier movement—if indeed there'd been any—might have been an animal.

I shrugged.

It was just another symptom, a return to paranoia, for me to imagine anything more sinister than a deer, moving along a well-traveled path. Another walker, not wanting solitude shattered. Or perhaps young lovers?

Certainly, I wasn't going to turn back. Especially since, my senses intensified by the careful search, I'd caught the distant murmur of rushing water.

"Me tired!" Pam whispered as I picked her up. "Mommy go home now?"

"Soon," I promised. "Mommy wants to see the water. Hear it? Maybe we'll see fish there!"

"Pammie want fishes," she said, but yawned.

She was asleep long before I passed the gentle stream—where fish did, indeed, move in darting patterns of silver—and neared a gorge where water ran, swift and violent, over rocks worn smooth as pavement. Here the sound was a roar, signaling a longer stretch of stream than I'd imagined.

But further exploration would have to be postponed. My arms throbbed with Pam's sleeping weight, and shadows—though still not dusk-long—were deepening. There was just the edge of evening chill to the air as I passed through the denser areas, and my heart beat a bit faster as I thought of getting home, preparing dinner, and waiting for Arden's call.

Long before we reached the spot where I'd sketched, I was wishing the bananas and cakes safely back in the kitchen. Once we'd entered the woods, Pam hadn't even mentioned eating, and I'd nearly forgotten, until the additional weight produced an almost audible ache in the bones and muscles of my arms and shoulders. And from the sketching spot on, there'd be the drawing pad and pastels to carry, too.

At least I could rest there.

Even at a distance, the flapping paper alarmed me. I'd thought the stones heavy enough to hold the sketchpad cover against the rising breeze, and now hoped fervently that the sketch hadn't smudged.

Hurrying down the final slope, I jarred Pam nearly awake. She murmured, "Mommy."

Then a flapping fragment careened away.

I slowed, seeing the breeze-swept paper—knowing that someone had been there. The pages had been held too tightly in the ring-bound pad for one to have ripped loose in anything less than a gale.

Even though somewhat prepared, I still reeled when I saw the sketch, torn raggedly again and again. All the pieces except the one that had blown away lay together, weighted by the stones I'd used. Someone had taken care that the sketch not be lost. That I know what had happened to it.

But who? Who that I knew, or didn't know, could want to hurt me by vandalizing my work? Or was this a warning?

I shuddered. Was it possible that someone intended harm not to me, but to *Pam?*

Involuntarily, my arms tightened about her. My throat ached, my pulse pounded, my eyes filled with tears in the need to protect her—a need surely intensified by the memory, still painful when touched, of my deepest-depression fear that I, myself, might do her harm.

"Please," I'd begged Arden, "please, if you hear me getting up in the night—follow me. I'm afraid I'll hurt . . . someone."

"Honey, you never could."

"Not when I'm *me*! I know that! But mothers have—when they're not themselves."

"Not you. Never you!"

"Just promise me. Promise!"

And he'd promised.

Other memories hounded me as I walked slowly back toward town. The day I'd told the psychiatrist—the first one, not dear Dr. David—about this fear.

He'd leaned back in his chair, totally unconcerned, lacking in empathy. "I wouldn't worry about it, Mrs. Templeton. When a woman kills her children, she usually makes it a package deal and kills herself as well."

Small comfort, that. I'd been considering suicide, too.

I was so numbed by my emotions, by the torn sketch, the memories, the physical weariness, that the healing accomplished by the walk and the sketching might never have occurred.

Heavily, I approached the back of the parsonage, looming in dusk-light.

Lelia waited for me on the porch steps. "I thought you might be out walking. I almost came looking for you." She moved quickly toward me, reaching for Pam. "You look exhausted!"

"I am." I tried to smile. "She's a heavy little critter."

"But sweet."

"Yes. Sweet." I moved slowly up the steps and into the house. The teakettle simmered gently on the stove, and I smelled fresh nut bread. I turned, smiling genuinely. "And so are you. Sweet."

She flushed. "I'd hoped you wouldn't mind."

"A steaming kettle and nut bread? Never!"

"I know you don't need me tonight. But could I stay a little while?"

"I'd love it! Stay and have supper with us, and then, if you wouldn't mind, you might watch Pam while I go to the hospital to visit Angie."

"Wonderful! And . . . if you don't want to be alone, I could stay overnight."

I touched her arm. "Much as I do appreciate it—no thanks." And only part of my refusal, I realized, as I went to release Fritz from his unaccustomed bondage, was that I felt the need to exert independence.

More importantly, when Arden called, I didn't want to share him with anyone.

CHAPTER 13

By 10:30 that evening, Arden still hadn't called, and a storm was moving in quickly from the north.

When I'd returned from visiting Angie, Lelia had made the rounds with me, locking church, annex, and parsonage doors, before she went home shortly before 9:00. Pam was already tucked in; Fritz slept before the murmuring TV. I sat down to relax with a book.

Then I heard the wind pick up and the storm approaching.

Not really minding the drumrolls of distant thunder or the rising wind, sounding like muted stringed instruments as it flowed through heavy, tossing branches, I went to the window, watched glimmers of distant lightning—and recalled my visit with Angie.

Ted had been there, looking a bit uncomfortable as her mother dominated the conversation and her attention. But it had been a pleasant visit. Angie had obviously been surprised to see me, and sorry that Arden wasn't along. When she asked about Pam, her smile was warm, her eyes dreamy; her hand strayed gently to the approximate location of her baby.

Mrs. Kleigh had been friendly, too, although I'd noticed lines of weariness and strain on her face, and a certain rigidity in her tone when she addressed a remark to Ted.

But surely, surely, that would pass.

Nature's orchestration approached crescendo. My mother, terrified of lightning, had always herded my unwilling brother, my sister, and me before her into any tiny spot of presumed safety, and cowered there herself, with us, until the last small sounds of thunder had died away. But Aunt Claudia had exulted in storms. The summer I'd spent in her Ohio home, she insisted that I watch with her as the dark sky boiled and festered with violent clouds, as trees and bushes responded to nature's heavy hand with a kind of sturdy pride. A flexibility. Their tossed plumage and shaken boughs seemed to issue their own challenge.

"That's how we must face life, child," my aunt had said, though she knew that at sixteen I was certainly no longer a child. "Your mother runs and hides—and I expect she's taught you to whimper, too. But life has no respect for cowards or dishrags, and if I have my way, you'll be neither."

And Aunt Claudia *had* made a difference, that short summer she'd dedicated to teaching me pride and independence and resilience and spunk. But the next winter, she'd fought cancer of the liver with her heads-up brand of courage. And lost.

I never watched a storm but I remembered Aunt Claudia and sent up a prayer of gratitude for having known her touch, however brief, on my life. If she'd lived longer, who knows what wonders she might have wrought? She might even have managed to dent my fear of heights.

Aunt Claudia would never have stood still for emotional breakdown—though Mother insisted that she was, and always had been, "crazy." Aunt Claudia wouldn't be waiting, as I was, each cell ready to respond to the ringing of the phone. Instead, she'd be off somewhere reading poetry—or writing it—papering a room or playing the piano and singing, loudly, off-key.

And she would not have allowed herself to feel threatened.

If her work had been destroyed, as mine had been, she'd have stalked through the whole woods—the entire county, if necessary—to find the culprit and force him to eat the torn fragments, with a piece of her mind for dessert.

Dear, marvelous, starchy Aunt Claudia. She was what Arden would call a "gutsy lady."

Arden.

As I glanced at the clock, the electricity flicked off and on again, in an instant.

Much as I enjoyed watching a storm, I hadn't bargained for a night alone without electricity.

Why hadn't he called?

Eleven o'clock.

Surely, by now, he'd be going to bed. The district superintendent always scheduled meeting days full, beginning shortly after first light.

Why don't you call, Arden? You promised to call.

Lightning flashed perilously close, illuminating tossing trees. And even before the thunder had acknowledged it, the lights flashed off again. The TV fell totally silent; the house crackled with quietness. In his sleep, Fritz must have sensed it, for I heard him rouse and whimper.

"Here I am," I said, just before the lights came on again. And the TV, its picture uncertain. I switched it off, unplugging it. I hadn't been watching, anyway, and if all I wanted was sound, I had it, stereophonically, just outside.

The rain began a slashing assault on the north windows. Soon the windows on all sides were sheathed in rain, like liquid glass. In a strange way, rather than being threatened by the storm, I felt protected. The house was encased with rain—sliding, slapping—an impregnable shield against intrusion.

I curled up on the couch and enjoyed it, until the lights extinguished again—firmly and finally. Even then, I didn't mind for a while. They'd come on soon, and I'd find a flashlight or candles.

But when they didn't—and time still moved on, measured only by quartz clocks in darkness—I began to determine my geographical relationship to the phone (for when Arden would call) and the flashlight. Where would Arden have left it? Or had he taken it with him? In the city, we'd kept it in the lower drawer of the desk. But there, the study had been downstairs, where here—

The phone shrilled into my thoughts.

Awkwardly, scrambling to my feet, I bumped my shin agonizingly against the coffee table. Disentangling myself, I lost precious seconds through two more rings,

"Don't hang up," I whispered. "Don't hang up. Don't hang up."

On the sixth ring, I got it.

"Arden!" I said, not waiting for his greeting. "I was afraid you weren't going to call after all! We're having the most terrific storm here. Are you?" I waited for his reply. "Arden?" Another pause. "Are you still there, Ar—"

But the laughter had begun, and I stood numbly, holding the receiver far from me, hoping that neither my anguish nor my anger could communicate itself to this obscene person, whoever it was, who'd dared to intercept the excitement, the joy, the love intended for Arden.

Sometime later—much, much later—I crawled upstairs, in the dark, to bed. Fritz accommodated his usual gamboling gait to mine, accompanied me to Pam's bed to listen to her even breathing, and slept just outside my door.

Throughout the night, the storm continued—at times, almost a benediction. At others, a violence. Several times I woke, thinking I'd heard sounds just outside. Or even within the house. But my sleep-drugged emotions were immune to terror. Safe within my cocoon of wind and rain, I slept again.

I woke to sunshine and restored electricity.

While breakfast cooked, Fritz took his run and returned, happily muddy. Quickly, I turned the stove heat to low and banished him to the basement. Crestfallen, he suffered himself to be led. But not without grumbling comment.

Then, halfway down the cellar stairs, his yips turned to a low growl.

I'd been looking at the steps, intent on our safe descent. Now, hearing the dog's warning, I looked up—and froze on the bottom step.

A figure hung from a floor support. A caricature of me. The scarf knotted about its mop-head hair was my scarf— one I kept for cleaning days or for outdoor work in the wind. Its skirt was my flowered wraparound; its blouse, my white peasant blouse—both left in the dryer the day before. The face on the pillowcase head was graphic—one sketched blue eye doll-wide, the other shut, with long lashes curling close to a pink-tinged cheek. A red-mitten tongue—Pam's mitten—lolled from the yarn-stitched mouth. A clothesline noose was knotted closely about the neck, then hung from the nail that usually held the clothespin bag.

Below the curious figure—somehow more chilling because of its comic qualities—stood my winter boots, one upright, one turned over.

Those boots, I knew, had been in the old footlocker in the corner of the cellar, brought straight from the city, where winter things had been packed away weeks before we'd known that we were to be uprooted.

For long moments I stood, unmoving.

Then Fritz, initiating a barking attack on the stranger in our basement, broke the spell.

I moved slowly from the bottom step to the cement floor.

An effigy—of me.

I'd never been hung in effigy before.

Unexpectedly, I began to laugh—a low, rumbling laugh, gaining in pitch and intensity, mounting, mounting, until, laughter and tears mingling, I leaned against the stair-rail, my shoulders shaking uncontrollably.

Fritz ceased his barking and licked my hand.

Glad for his comfort, for any comfort, I eased myself down onto the bottom step. Still crying, I sat there, rubbing his head, his ears.

"Oh, Fritz. Oh, Arden! Oh, dear, dear God—"

And then the phone shrilled.

Listening through two rings, I tried to tug myself from my hysteria to a saner reality.

It must be Arden.

It must be.

Unless it was my other caller, who might very well be responsible for this . . . whatever it was, mockery or warning.

Woodenly, I pulled myself to my feet and mounted the stairs.

The phone was on the seventh ring. The eighth.

I couldn't have moved quickly if the steps had broken into flame beneath my feet.

At first, it seemed that Fritz would go with me. Then, halfway up, he stopped and sat on the step, barking at the other me.

The ninth ring. Tenth. Eleventh.

I picked it up on the twelfth.

"Oh, Arden," I said dully. "Oh, Arden."

But what if it wasn't Arden?

I waited.

"Honey!" His voice was sharp. "What is it?"

"Oh, Arden." I swallowed hard. "You didn't call last night."

"I tried, honey. I'm really sorry. The phones were out here. We had a terrible storm."

"So did we. That's what I started to tell you when you called last night—only it was just someone else. Laughing. That we were having a terrific storm, I mean. Aunt Claudia would have loved it."

"Is . . . everything all right, Paula?" he asked. "You weren't frightened of the storm, were you?"

"I loved it. Like Aunt Claudia." I could hear my voice. Monotonous. Strange. He'd be sure that I was slipping back.

And maybe I was. I choked on a sob. That thing in the cellar—

"Honey," he said, very calmly. Very Arden-like. "Honey, tell me what's wrong."

"Oh, Arden. Oh, Fritz—"

"Fritz. It's Fritz? Something's happened to Fritz?"

"He's in the basement, barking. Can't you hear him? Here, listen." I held the receiver away, then brought it back. "Did you hear him?"

"I think so. What's he barking about?"

"Oh, Arden . . ."

"Honey. Honey." And his voice was agonized. "Not Pam—" He drew a long breath. I could hear it wavering over the distance, and I drew one, too, and truly tried to get myself back together, to assure him that Pam was all right. That *I* was all right.

Only, how could I be all right with that thing—that obscenity—hanging in the basement?

And the tears began again, and the laughter, as I sank into a deep chair and tumbled the story in jumbled fragments that must have sounded to him like the insanity I had never quite achieved before, but had been working on.

He said at last, dully, "I'll tell Dr. Connelly I need to leave early."

"No. Wait," I begged. "I'm all right, Arden, really I am. It's only that I'd just discovered it when the phone rang. And I wasn't over the shock. But I'm calm now."

"Good girl," he said. "Now, slow down and tell me again. There was something in the basement. I got that much. Something—hanging?"

"It was *me*!" I said, the laughter/tears shaking me again. "Supposed to be *me*! My skirt, my blouse, my blue eye— staring—an *effigy*, Arden!" I finished, my voice strangling. "Of *me*!"

"An ef—" That long sigh again. "Honey, you're sure."

"Do you think I could make up something like that? Even at my worst, for heaven's sake?"

"Okay, honey. Okay. I'm sorry. It's just—you know the way light is in dim places sometimes. And when we look at something quickly, it can seem like something else. I remember when I was a kid, one time, waking up and thinking there were giant bugs crawling over my walls. I was terrified. But all it was—my mother explained when she heard me screaming—were the shadows of leaves from outside my window. The moon was very bright, and the wind moving the leaves—"

I sighed. "You'd like for me to go and look again."

"Could you? Get someone to go with you. Lelia, maybe?"

"I don't need Lelia or anyone else to tell me what I see."

He laughed, without humor. "Even me, I know. But I didn't mean to take her along for—for a *witness*. I meant you might want her there just in case you're—"

"Frightened? I'm not frightened, Arden. Not anymore. I'll admit, when I saw it—" I paused. "But I'm not frightened now. Just furious."

"I understand, honey. Really, I do. But you *will* go, right? And I'll wait, right here."

Carefully, I laid down the receiver, but his voice called me back. "Make sure the outside cellar door's locked," he said grimly. "And prop something under the doorknob."

I murmured agreement.

Fritz had stopped barking, I noticed.

Quickly, purposefully, I moved through the kitchen toward the basement stairs, and—bracing myself for what hung there, below—started down.

Moments later I was back, panting, a scream begging for utterance. My hands trembled as I took up the receiver. Knees buckling beneath me, I sank toward the floor and rested my head against the welcome stability of the table edge.

"Oh, Arden," I whispered. "Arden—horrible, horrible!"

His voice was tense. "Then it really was there."

"Oh, yes, it really was there—just as I told you—" My voice broke on a sob. "But not now, Arden. Not now. Now—it's gone . . ."

I had stared unbelieving at the clothes-pin bag, swinging just a bit from its accustomed nail. My boots were gone—shoved, I had no doubt, into the footlocker in the corner. I'd known without looking that my blouse and skirt would be in the dryer. Pam's mitten—yes, on the windowsill, where I remembered laying it for safety as we'd moved things into the basement. One single mitten, waiting until I could find its mate—but no hurry, not until winter.

Only the pillowcase face unaccounted for. Where was the pillowcase? I'd thrown things out of the dryer, searching. Rummaged in the locker (yes, of course, my boots were there), and prowled behind the freezer, even opening the lid and peering in.

No pillowcase.

And no time to look further, since Arden was waiting on the line to be told that he'd been right all the time, that it was just my imagination. Again.

"It was there," I'd said through gritted teeth. "I know what I saw."

Fritz, at peace again with his environment, had flicked his tail and cocked an ear, not following as I'd run up the stairs.

Arden's voice was strangely deep. "Honey . . . you did check the cellar door?"

I hadn't, of course. "But I will."

"And you've got to ask Lelia to stay."

I sighed.

"I . . . I could come home."

"No," I said. "I don't need you." And I hung up.

CHAPTER 14

By the time Lelia arrived, half an hour or so later, I had myself under control again. I'd fed Pam, washed her dishes, and once more—though more calmly—searched the basement for the pillowcase.

Of course I hadn't found it.

But it was there, I told myself and God. *It was there. We both know it was there.*

Even Arden, I suspected, had half believed.

Fritz would know, too, I thought resentfully, as he panted foolishly in Pam's wake. And he'd know who it was who had left the outside cellar door slightly ajar—someone who had a key, one of any number who had a key, and who had perhaps been hiding, laughing silently while waiting through my frenzy—someone who'd worked feverishly to restore order while Arden tried to calm me. Someone Fritz knew? Someone he wouldn't challenge. Foolish thought. He wouldn't have challenged anyone!

Lelia asked quietly, "Is everything all right?"

"Fine," I answered woodenly, and followed with a wooden smile. She read to Pam for a while, then came to the kitchen where I was preparing to bake cherry pie, Arden's favorite, but not for Arden. For the Women's Society meeting.

"Our electricity was off last night," she said. "Almost three and a half hours."

"Ours, too."

And, so I wouldn't forget, I looked for the flashlight and found it in a kitchen cupboard. I set it within easy reach, near the microwave.

"Did everything go all right?"

"I like storms."

"*Do* you?" She leaned forward, hands clasped, studying me as though I might be a specimen in a lab.

I laughed. My mother had reacted similarly, that summer I'd returned from Aunt Claudia's. I paused. "When Arden called, he insisted I ask you to stay with us tonight."

"I'll be glad to." She frowned. "You really don't want me, though."

"If someone has to stay, I'm happy it's you!" I shrugged. "I just think he's being over-protective." Remembering the effigy, I stiffened. Should I tell Lelia—

But she was saying softly, "People protect the ones they love. That's rather wonderful, don't you think?"

I relaxed, smiling. "Yes," I agreed, "that's very wonderful." And I felt guilty about baking the pie when he wouldn't be there to share it.

I'd expected the day to drag, as the day before had, but it didn't. And I'd expected the fear of the morning to color every moment—but forgot for blocks of time before that image would recur, jarring me.

But the outside cellar door was secure, now—locked and braced. And though there were other doors . . . still, somehow, calmness returned to allow a kind of normalcy.

First there was the Women's Society meeting, scheduled for 11:30 in the annex. By the time the pie was out of the oven, it was time to dress for that.

"Are you going?" I asked Lelia.

She shrugged. "I'd rather have an excuse not to."

"Like Pam?"

She grinned conspiratorially.

"Consider yourself excused."

She reached out, gathering a giggling, squirming Pam into her lap, and we laughed together. With her cheek cuddled in Pam's hair, she said, "It's just that—" A broad gesture concluded the thought.

"I don't like meetings either," I confided.

"But—?"

"But I'm a minister's wife?"

She nodded.

I leaned closer, whispering, "We're human, too."

"Even if you do like storms," she teased, then, sobering, "What I hate most is the gossip. They're so . . . sanctimonious about it. As though they really care about the person they're ripping apart. As though they're doing it in Christian love."

"Probably some of them are."

"But most are just licking their lips. And thanking God that *they're* above such things."

I sank carefully to the sofa edge. "You sound as though you've been touched by it."

"They thought I was too little to understand, but I knew they were talking about—"

"Your mother?" I asked gently, reaching out to stroke her hair. Lightly, as she was stroking Pam's.

Childlike tears welled into her eyes. "Once, I'd had more than I could stand. So I really told them off. Grandmother was furious with me."

My hand stilled. "With *you*?"

"I . . . was defending my dad." She swallowed noisily. "So I came over here. I can't even remember who was here then—but it seemed to be the only place I could find comfort. Ever."

I had no answer, so I just sat quietly, near her, until it was time to go.

First, though, I went to the basement and tested the chair, propped under the doorknob.

I noticed the odor as soon as I opened the door between the parsonage and the annex kitchen. Subconsciously, I suppose, I recognized it at once as paint. And perhaps, subconsciously, I knew what that would mean.

Just short of entering the meeting room, I knew with my conscious mind as well, and stopped short, bracing myself.

It must have been done earlier that morning, while Lelia and I worked and talked in the kitchen. Only one coat, so far. In spots, the mural glowed through, and the black lines—most of them—were still discernible.

I knew anger as I'd known it the day before when my sketch of Pam had been torn. As I'd experienced it that morning when my personality had been violated by the creation of that effigy.

This anger, though, was perhaps the most vivid of the three, for I felt it for Dean, who stood just inside the annex door, his shoulders slumped, his face at first empty of expression, then hardening through grief to hatred. And the hatred, it seemed, was for me. He turned it toward me in its full intensity, then stalked from the room.

Running after him, I called his name. But his shoulders only grew more rigid, and his pace quickened.

There'd been chatter in the room when I'd first entered. It had ceased abruptly when I'd called Dean's name. Now it ebbed and flowed again, almost naturally, as quilting needles plied themselves in expert, neat little stitches across rows of Dresden plates. Only Mrs. Bancroft sat quietly, grim-lipped, obviously uncomfortable, jabbing her needle in vicious little strokes as though she would like to kill it. Or someone.

"Mrs. Templeton!" Minnie Kelp called buoyantly. "There you are! We were wondering when you'd finally get here!"

Witch! I thought—and knew that Arden would be shocked. God, too. Though perhaps God, identifying with my empathy for Dean, would understand. I stood for another long moment, ostensibly watching Dean, but in reality weighing my alternatives.

I could make a scene, thus giving Minnie Kelp delight for long, lonely hours of gloating. At least an outburst would relieve my own feelings.

I could mention it briefly, then refuse to be drawn into further controversy. But I would still be seething inwardly.

Or I could ignore the subject entirely.

I decided on the last—and wondered if I could handle it.

Firmly, I made my way to them. "Ladies," I said, smiling at each of them. "Mrs. Bancroft, how are you this morning?"

Her eyes were shooting sparks. "Sit here beside me, dear," she invited. "There's room for both of us on the same side."

Her double-pointed statement wasn't lost on Minnie Kelp. Or on any of the others, two or three of whom looked shyly pleased.

And that wasn't lost on Minnie either.

Well, Minnie, old girl, I thought, looks as though you won't have everything going your way!

I settled back to enjoy my advantage, and hoped that God would understand that, too.

Arden called while I had my hands in dishwater, and I asked Lelia to get it. She talked quietly for a moment or two, then called me to the phone.

"Hi, honey! How did today go?" His voice sounded strained. Tired.

"Fine." I'd decided not to mention the mural. In fact, I

remembered, with something of a shock, I'd even forgotten to tell Lelia about it after the meeting.

"I'm glad you asked Lelia to stay."

"I got my orders."

After a pause, he said, "Honey—I don't mean to give orders."

"When will you be home?"

He sighed. "Sometime late. Really late, I'm afraid. Our final session's a dinner one. Some of the guys are staying over, then getting an early start the next morning—"

"Why don't you, if you want to?" Why was I being so perverse?

"I *don't* want to. I'll be home as soon as I can, but—"

"Yes, I'll ask her to stay until you get here. That was what you were going to ask, wasn't it?"

"Honey—"

I waited.

"I love you."

Another silence, and I let it grow, until finally someone had to say something. So I did. "I have dishes in the sink."

"Then—I'll see you tomorrow night."

"Late."

"But as early as I can make it."

And we hung up.

It wasn't until later, as I stood crying quietly over the dishes, that I remembered. I should have told him to drive carefully.

And there was no way I could call him back, either to tell him that, or to say that I loved him, too. And needed him.

Salty tears splashed into the suds, killing one bubble at a time.

We walked outside, Pam and Lelia and I, and watched the sunset. Except for Pam's chatter, we were silent as the sky turned violet, then magenta, then gold. I was so deep in my own thoughts that I failed to see Dean until he—obviously wanting to avoid me—crossed the street and set off at a jogging pace.

"Dean!" I called.

His pace broke, then intensified.

"*Dean!*" and, when he didn't stop, "I'll run you down if I have to!"

He stopped, turned, a grin warring with his defensiveness. "You couldn't, not in a million years!" His chest expanded. "Even the Rev couldn't catch me!"

Before, I thought regretfully, such pride had been invested in his mural. I waited until I'd reached him, until I could touch his arm.

He flinched only slightly.

"Dean. I didn't do it."

He squirmed, and I tightened my grip.

"I figured that out almost right away," he said, looking anywhere but toward me. "It was your work, too." His voice deepened, and he peered searchingly, directly into my eyes. "Artists can't destroy their own work. Why would anybody else want to?"

It was my turn to look away. Why, indeed? And, without planning to, my mind turned to my sketch of Pam, destroyed in the woods. I shivered.

"You ain't cold, are you?" he asked. "'Cause . . . maybe we could talk in the church."

There was such yearning in his voice, in his expression, that I nodded. If only Arden were there! He'd recognize the direction of Dean's emotional and spiritual needs. He'd know, instinctively, how much to say. When to stop. I'd never felt comfortable witnessing with words, and Dean's soul was too fragile, too valuable, to risk with clumsiness. Or to risk in delay.

Any soul was.

I glanced toward Lelia, and she nodded. Smiled. How quickly understanding had grown between us! My heart warmed, then turned to sighing as I remembered Lelia's wounds. Instead of concentrating on helping her heal hers, I had merely allowed her to cushion mine.

Only remnants of sunset gold ignited the stained-glass windows. I reached for a light switch, but Dean tugged me past the sanctuary. To the annex.

Of course. He'd want to mourn the death of the mural. With that I felt more comfortable.

We sat in the duskiness of nearing night. The second-coated wall gleamed, but only slight strands of odor remained.

Dean sighed and leaned forward, elbows to his knees. "I can still almost see it."

"The black's stubborn. And the texture still shows. If we wanted to, we could still follow the lines."

His face brightened, then dimmed. "They'd only paint over it again."

He was right. "But maybe later. Sometimes, if we're patient, people's hearts change."

"Hers won't." He gave me a sideways glance. "I know who done it."

"Oh, Dean." I touched his shoulder, and he allowed me.

"It's okay. As soon as I knew it hadn't been you—or the Rev—I could handle it." His voice deepened. "I've had t' handle worse'n that."

I could think of no response.

"And it ain't really gone."

"The news photo?" I asked quietly.

His eyebrow arched in what might have been disappointment. "More than that. It's . . . in here," and he placed his hand over his heart, almost reverently.

I felt bumbling. Humbled.

"In a way," he said awkwardly, "it was kinda—" He broke off, cleared his throat, and began again. "At first, it was gettin' back at the Rev. But you knew that. And then, when we was workin' at it, it was sort of—you know. Us, together, watching something beautiful happen."

"I felt it, too."

He smiled. "I knew that." He cleared his throat and fidgeted. "Then there was the big ego thing, with the newspaper article, and I walked around for a while as though I was first cousin to God." He grinned at me, shyly. "You saw that, too."

"It's forgivable. A creator always feels kinship with *the* Creator."

"Yeah."His expression showed genuine understanding. "Then, after the swelling in my head went down, I felt real small. And grateful. And the mural became—sort of—my gift to Him."

"Oh, Dean." The tears were in my voice, as well as in my eyes. How often I'd known that progression in my own emotions! My hand tightened on his shoulder, and I felt an aching need to reach out, to strengthen the kinship.

And when I hugged him, it was I—still wary of scaring him off—who pulled away first.

I needn't have worried.

"Could we go to the other part of the church now?" he asked. "I'd like to tell Him what I just told you."

Of course God already knew and rejoiced. But recognizing how important it was—both for Dean and for God—that Dean put it into his own words, I followed without speaking.

Thank You, God. The prayer swelled my heart. *And thanks for letting it be me.*

Somehow, I thought that Arden might not, after all, have sensed the direction Dean needed to move. For all his pastoral gifts and insights, Arden lacked the artist's peculiar sensitivity.

Pam was in bed by the time I'd checked all the sanctuary and annex locks and returned to the parsonage. Lelia glanced up from watching TV, then studied me intently. "You look happy!"

"I am happy!"

She waited, and I wanted to share the reason—but with Arden, first. Besides, it was too fresh and momentous, yet, to shape itself into words.

Sighing, Lelia turned back to the television.

"Thanks for watching Pam."

She nodded.

"You've been spending as much time with her as I have! Maybe even more."

Her expression softened.

"Suddenly, I need some popcorn!" I said.

"Pam might still be awake!"

I laughed. "If she isn't, she will be, as soon as the smell of popcorn tickles her nose."

"I'll get her!"

"And I'll dig out the corn popper." But first I went to the basement one more time, to make certain the chair was secure beneath the doorknob. *Compulsive, compulsive,* I accused myself, but—as Dr. David would have said it—without rancor.

It was a comfortable, cozy evening, and I was still smiling as I prepared for bed.

The phone rang, and even knowing that it might be Arden again, I braced myself.

I lifted the receiver after the second ring, my heart lurching.

"I'm sorry to call so late," a light voice said. "Did I waken you?"

"I was just getting ready for bed."

"So was I. But then I remembered that I hadn't called you yet to thank you for coming to see me. In the hospital."

"Angie!"

"Yeah."

"You're home?"

"Yeah. But that's not the only reason—"

"You're happy," I said.

"I knew it would show! Even over the phone!" She giggled. "Things are going so well. Rev. Templeton was right. All it took was some time, and the love—" Her voice broke but mended quickly. "We want your husband to marry us. Our folks do, too."

"Angie, I'm so happy! He will be, too—and I'll have him call you when he gets back."

"Oh, that's right. You mentioned, at the hospital, that he was out of town."

"I'll have him call you day after tomorrow," I said.

"I can't wait to talk to him! And I'm sorry we didn't stay for church on Sunday."

"It was an uncomfortable time. For everyone."

"Yeah. But Ted and I both said later we shoulda stayed. To show we're on his side. But he'll know, won't he, when you tell him about the wedding." She gave me no time to respond as she rushed on in a squealing, little-girl voice, "The wedding! I can't believe it! Even the word sounds beautiful!"

She didn't wait for my assurance or my good-bye but hung up on that note of high excitement. I could picture her, sitting cross-legged on her bed, hugging herself. And drifting, slowly through her excitement, into a dream of endless love and sharing and joy.

Of course, life wouldn't be like that. It wasn't for anyone. But for Ted and Angie, it just might come impossibly close.

I prayed so as I drifted into my own comfortable dreams.

CHAPTER 15

My first waking thought was of Arden's return. My second was of Angie and Ted. And my third of Dean.

I stretched broadly.

How could it not be a great day!

When the phone rang, I picked it up quickly. Confidently. It was Dee.

"I can tell by the lilt in your voice that you're feeling better!" she said.

"Are you working already?"

"Just thinking about it. And about you."

"I'm sorry I worried you."

"What are friends for?"

"I'm afraid I haven't been easy on my friends lately." Or on my husband, I thought, and winced.

"Well, the first time a prize-winning pot breaks in the kiln, I'll allow you to give me therapy."

"No greater tragedy than that," I said lightly—but thought of Dean's grief over the mural. Of my anguish over the effigy. "Of course, it's the tragedies that bring the growth." I hadn't meant to say that and wished I hadn't when I noticed her sudden silence.

I laughed. "Just philosophizing."

"Still, you sounded solemn. And before—"

"Before, I sounded the way I feel today! It's bright and sunny out—"

"It's raining here."

"Well, then, you can shut yourself into the studio and create works of undying value."

"Ha. If I do, for sure this will be the 'Day of the Tragedy in the Kiln'!"

"Then you'll just have to call me again!"

"And . . . will you still be feeling great?"

"Guaranteed!"

Apparently I'd convinced her, because she said something about summoning her Muse and hung up after a breezy good-bye.

I stretched again.

It was going to be a great day!

We were finishing breakfast when the phone rang again.

"Amy Turkle," the bright voice said. "I'm the mother of a new poem and thought you might like to go for a walk in the woods later."

The woods. I sighed.

"It's such a gorgeous day, and there's a special place I want to show you." Her next words were clouded. "Turk and I used to go there . . ."

The woods. When I passed the place where the ruined sketch had flapped in the breeze, wouldn't my day descend into gloom?

But if I began avoiding that lovely area, wouldn't I be transforming my enemy, whoever it was, into a victor?

"I'll go," I said.

"If you don't want to—" She must have sensed my hesitancy.

"I do!"

"Fine! Bring that sweet little Pam along."

"Lelia's staying with her today."'

"Bring Lelia, too! In an hour?"

"We'll be ready."

The woods were cool and inviting, with splatters and splays and smudges of sunlight everywhere. Pam tried to catch the flecks of brilliance that danced with each sparse movement of leaves. Fritz chased after rabbits, who sought sanctuary among the giant roots; squirrels, who regarded him disdainfully from swaying branches; and, eventually, in a long-dry streambed, a toad he seemed to prefer harassing rather than catching.

Lelia walked slowly, thoughtfully, with characteristic quietness. I wondered what thoughts absorbed her and hoped they weren't fears of depression, echoing our conversation of—how long ago had it been? I flushed with the knowledge that I'd been so caught up in my own concerns that I hadn't broached the subject again with her, and promised myself that I would. Later. After the walk.

Amy led us along the bank of the living stream, past rapids, to a quiet place where the water, widening, pooled benignly.

"Beautiful!" I whispered.

"There's more. It turns violent again, just a short distance away."

"There's a swinging bridge," Lelia contributed, and I found myself surprised that she'd been listening. "It's at least a hundred feet above a gorge. And nearly that long."

I shivered.

Amy laughed. Her eyes sparkled, and I could scarcely notice the bruise Arden had mentioned. "Don't tell me you're acrophobic!"

"Terminally."

Lelia threw me such an intent look that I squirmed inwardly. But she said nothing, and I was sure that, still deep in her thoughts, she hadn't realized how closely she'd regarded me.

But then she said, "My father was afraid of height, too," and she walked more quickly, moving at an angle to intercept Pam's path. Pam reached up her arms to be carried, and Lelia, smiling, made a huge show of lifting such a heavy burden, while Pam giggled with delight. Leaving the two of them counting caterpillars, Amy and I walked a bit further before settling down onto a large rock.

Her poem was lovely, as the others had been, but with such a deep, understated yet pervasive sadness that I sighed.

"I know," she said. "And yet, once I'd written it, I felt as light as air."

I'd experienced that feeling often, having drained anger or fear onto a canvas.

I wanted to say so many things to her. *Your life is so sad. How can I help? Or . . . Please let me be your friend. Please let me do for you what Dee has done for me.*

But there was no comparison between Amy's problem and mine. How could anyone help? Except, I thought grimly, by taking out a contract on Turk.

"I loved him so much," she said.

Past tense, I noted.

"Once in a while, I think I still do. And then he laughs at me and rips me down to nothing again."

"He's afraid." I was as startled as she, wondering where the words had come from. Afraid of what? I wondered.

"Afraid of what?" she asked.

"I . . . I read somewhere once that a bully always acts from fear."

She said drily, "Well, he's a bully all right. But everyone else does the fearing."

I watched her draw circles on the ground with the toe of her sneaker. She looked so pensive, so vulnerable, I longed for my sketchbook to try to capture her there. I wanted to reach out and touch her—gently.

But Turk had touched her gently once. And then reduced her to emotional shambles.

And another thought came. A question . . . and then not a question, but a certainty. "He's afraid of losing you."

She frowned. "He's already lost me."

"He doesn't realize that."

"He will. Later today." She pulled a second folded fragment of paper from her pocket.

"Another poem?"

"I wrote it after I called you."

The lines were poignant with good-bye. With love lost, faith destroyed, hope in a future alone.

"He'll find it after I'm gone."

"Oh, Amy!" I hugged her then. "I'll miss you so."

She was about to say something further when both of us, apparently at the same instant, reacted to voices. Pam's and Lelia's, approaching in waves of excitement and enchantment.

Amy stood, brushing off fragments of bark and dead moss. "I'd better get back. I have a lot to do before . . . " she glanced toward Lelia, "before Turk gets home."

I gave her a quick hug, watched as she smiled at Lelia and bent to kiss Pam, and listened until her hurrying footsteps faded to silence.

"That Turk," Lelia said tightly, recapturing my attention. "How could anyone ever love someone like him?"

We began to walk slowly toward home. "Maybe he wasn't always like that."

"Maybe not as cruel as he is now. But he was sure of his good looks and his strength and his importance even when he was Dean's age."

I waited.

"Grandmother says he's just like my father, but she's wrong!" Her face contorted, and she turned slightly away to dab at her eyes.

Neither of us spoke until we'd left the stream behind us. Pam, shuffling along now on her little legs, seemed too weary for speech. I picked her up, and she snuggled against my neck.

New pain touched Lelia's eyes.

"Would you like to carry her?" I asked.

"Not unless you're too tired." Her voice, like her posture, was stiff.

Pam's arms relaxed, and her breathing grew heavy. Deep. Measured.

"Besides," Lelia whispered, "she's already asleep." She smiled. "Sorry I'm such a grouch."

Our silence became companionable.

"Lelia . . ."

She turned.

We'd reached the edge of the woods, maneuvered past the tangled wire. She squinted into full sunlight.

"I . . . I feel so selfish that I haven't asked how you're doing."

She looked away. "Things are so much better that I don't feel like the same person!" She paused. "Honestly."

I couldn't help but wish that she'd looked at me as she spoke. Still, she sounded sincere.

She stooped to pick a violet. "You've helped me. A lot. To know that you've been through the blackness and come out of it so well . . . it proved I can do it. I just have to make up my mind to do whatever it takes to make things perfect."

I said slowly, "Things are never really perfect, Lelia."

"Close enough." She looked directly into my eyes. "They are for you. And they will be for me, too. Soon."

Shocked, I wondered if Lelia planned to leave home, too. Then embarrassment surged through me. Perhaps leaving home was precisely what she should do to escape the sphere of recriminations, reminders of a past she'd had no part in shaping, and a present she had little power to alter as long as she remained in her grandmother's house.

Why had I reacted so strongly? Because this would be another of my own bulwarks gone? Recognition of my self-ishness warmed me even further to her cause. "If there's any way I can help . . ."

Unexpectedly, she hugged me—so tightly that Pam squirmed and murmured. Lelia's breath moved warmly on my cheek as she whispered, "You can't know how much I appreciate your considering me a friend."

Since it had been understood that Lelia would remain until Arden got home, I suggested that she stay the night again. Pam had gone home with her to "help" her pack another change of clothing.

I had macaroni stew nearly ready and was just waiting for their return when I heard a step on the porch.

A heavy step.

My heart jumped. Arden? Early?

No, too heavy for Arden.

Glancing up, I wished that I'd locked the outer door. Thoughts of the effigy jolted me.

Too late. Turk walked in without knocking.

I had seen him looking cruel. Mocking. Suggestive. But I'd never witnessed such anger as whitened his face and blazed from his eyes.

"*Where is she?*"

I needed time to think. "Lelia went—"

"*Not Lelia!*" But something new had invaded those fierce eyes, and I realized that I'd given away an advantage. He'd have known, of course, that Arden wasn't home. Now he knew that, except perhaps for Pam, I was alone.

Involuntarily, I took a backward step. Thank God Pam was safe!

He moved that one step closer. "I found her note."

"Then . . . surely she told you—"

"Oh, it told me enough, all right! It told me suddenly I ain't good enough for her." Anguish twisted the line of his mouth, and my heart spoke to that vulnerability. Even in him.

"She *doesn't* feel that she's better than you."

He reacted to my softness with more venom than to my fear. "You seen her today—didn't you!" Lunging forward, he grasped my wrist in fingers that tightened. And tightened. And tightened.

When I gasped, victory lit his eyes again. Please, God, I thought, is there no way to break through this man's need to conquer? To give pain?

He repeated, more softly, his grip loosening ever so slightly, "You seen her." I could feel the brush of his clothing against mine. "And what poison did you feed her today, little Mrs. Reverend? Did you tell her God loves her more than I do? Did you give her th' line your gutless husband fed her— that's had her lookin' so . . . so . . ."

"Unafraid?" The word forced itself from between my stiff lips. "Is that why you're worried? That she won't cower from you any longer, like a puppy that's been whipped?"

Harshly, his fingers bit into my wrist, and he forced my hand backward.

I felt my breath tighten. And my resolve. Let him break my wrist, if that's what he wanted. I wouldn't let him see me afraid. Ever again.

I was wrong.

The skillet sizzled and spat on the stove, and the odors

of scorched tomato and macaroni pervaded the room. With his free hand, he reached to switch off the burner. "We don't want the house burnin' down around our ears, do we?" he asked softly. "Not when there's so much . . . unfinished business."

And that quickly he twisted my arm behind me and forced me toward the living room, dim with gathering dusk. Toward the couch.

Dear, God, help me, I prayed . . . but no recognizable help came. No confirmation of control. No power of speech to wheedle, to reason. And certainly no physical strength that could resist his.

My thoughts raced. *Arden . . . please come—now! Lelia!*

He shoved me onto the couch and pinioned my arms beneath me. Except for my face, which I'd turned away, I couldn't move.

And then, with one hand, he forced my face toward his. And he was smiling.

"It's only fair," he rationalized. "Ain't it? The preacher takes my woman. I take his."

I tried to squirm, and he laughed at my helplessness.

"He didn't take—"

He clamped a hand over my lips. "Oh, not in bed. That, I coulda understood. Worse—he took her mind." He moved his hand from my lips, to my shoulder, to . . .

I closed my eyes to shut out the terror. To better reach God with prayer.

"That's right. Just relax. It ain't *your* mind I'm after," and his lips closed over mine fiercely—splitting my lip against a tooth.

The prayer became a scream within me. A wrenching. *Please, God, help me!*

"We're here!"

Lelia! *Thank you, God!*

Turk chuckled lazily. He stood, taking my hand, tugging me to my feet—almost gallantly. "Now, don't you feel cheated," he whispered. "There'll come another time. Real soon."

He turned, still smiling, to Lelia and Pam who were now in the living room doorway. "She got a little dizzy," he said, "but she's feelin' much better, now. Ain't you, Mrs. Templeton?"

I forced a smile and a nod for Lelia. For Pam. For my own equilibrium. "Much better." My mouth framed the words, but no sound came. I tried again. "Much . . . better."

Throughout the meal, which was scarcely edible, I was aware of Lelia's questioning, concerned glances.

But it wasn't until we were clearing the table that she ventured, "That 'dizzy' thing didn't fool me a bit. Was he—I mean, he wasn't—"

Her face colored, and she wouldn't look at me.

She must not watch "The Flame and the Fury," I thought, half-smiling, or the terminology would come more easily.

"No," I said gently.

By then, I wasn't sure myself that he'd intended to rape me. For Turk, it might be more satisfying to produce the terror and the expectation than to fulfill the threat.

And yet, he'd killed the mouse.

Still, when the "mouse" was human, and capable of retaining the fear, and feeding it. . . . I wondered if he was subtle enough for effigies.

Anger flooded me. I would not allow Turk to victimize me. I was through being a victim. I felt my teeth clenching.

"I despise him, too," Lelia said. "It was such a perfect day, before."

I grasped at the promise. "We could make popcorn again."

"Pop-corn!" repeated Pam, hugging her teddy. "'Gain!"

"But later, okay?" Lelia suggested. "I feel the need for a long, leisurely shower. If you don't mind."

"The water's free!"

"We'll do the dishes first."

"No, you go ahead. I'll finish up here."

"Then I'll feed Fritz." She pulled the nearly empty bag of dog food from beside the refrigerator and hurried to the back porch.

Already, dusk was deepening.

"Take the flashlight," I said.

Chapter 16

Pam was washed up and in her nightclothes, the kitchen swept and straightened, and the dishes all but done, when Lelia entered from the darkness.

"I couldn't find Fritz anywhere." Her voice was husky with concern. "I called and called."

"He's probably chasing a rabbit." Still, it wasn't like Fritz to be missing at mealtime. "I'll look for him as soon as I get the burned macaroni off this skillet." I worked the scouring pad harder. "If I ever do." The scrubbing effort had intensified the pain in my wrist, where Turk's cruelty had left bruises.

"I could do it," Lelia offered.

"You go take your shower."

"I may read a few stories to Pammie first."

I smiled over my shoulder. "She'd love that."

When the skillet finally felt smooth again, I still heard the comforting drone of their voices. Taking the flashlight and a pocketful of dog food, I went to find Fritz.

The night was deep-dark. Only a slight glow at the horizon promised moonlight for later. Arden would be driving home through moonlight. The thought warmed me. Each moment brought him that much closer.

I kept him firmly in my thoughts, to allay other images the darkness might bring. Anything could lie beyond the small circle of light the flashlight threw. And anything—or anyone—could move just beyond its reach as I advanced.

"Fritz! Fritz!" My voice testified to greater peace than I felt. ("There'll come another time," Turk had promised. "Real soon.")

I ordered him from my thoughts. But memory of his mocking persisted. And my hatred deepened, though I knew that Arden would urge me to pray for him instead.

But prayer for Turk held low priority on such a night, with the darkness oozing everywhere and familiar shapes becoming strangers.

I searched, calling, all around the church and the block, then angled past the senior citizen housing toward the woods, until its bulk stood like a warning, just the length of a field away. My flashlight flickered. I turned it off, and keeping the lights of the parsonage in view, I continued on in darkness that was relieved only by an occasional anemic streetlight. When footsteps shuffled from the opposite sidewalk, my fingers tightened on the undependable flashlight.

"Mrs. Templeton?"

I laughed with relief. "Dean? What are you doing, walking around in the dark?"

He laughed. "You're kinda in the dark yourself."

"You're absolutely right! Just now, I'm saving batteries."

"Where you goin'?"

"I'm looking for Fritz. Have you seen him?" Strange, how much more secure I felt with his company.

"I seen him 'bout two hours ago. Chasin' a chipmunk."

"Not toward the woods again, I hope!"

"Toward the park. He looked tired."

The park. He was probably lying there, tail flicking, hoping to be ready when the chipmunk made itself available again.

"How far are we from the park?"

"Almost there." He laughed. "You ain't very good at

directions, are you?" He forgave me quickly. "'Course, I've lived here all my life."

That lovable pride again. Dear Dean. "Fritz!" I called.

"He ain't gonna hear that tiny whisper! FRITZ!" he yelled.

I felt him gathering himself for a louder shout, but stopped him with, "Maybe he's on the far side of the park?"

Occasionally, I risked the dying battery for a quick glimpse of the terrain ahead and on either side. No sign. Where was the moon, anyway? I glanced upward for the answer. Clouds.

I sighed. "Where could he be?"

"Maybe he run away?" Dean suggested.

"He never has before." I stumbled on a tree root, and he put his hand firmly under my arm to steady me. "Where are we now?"

"About two blocks from your place. You okay?"

"Fine. You're a good leader."

"Yeah," he agreed, and pulled me along a bit faster. "Fritz! Fritzie!" he called, and whistled piercingly.

And then I tripped over something.

"The sidewalk oughta be okay here," he said, helping me up.

It had been soft. Yielding. Perhaps a towel, dropped by one of the boys going home from swimming. I switched on the flickering light.

"Holy gee!" whistled Dean, dropping to one knee.

Knowing then why Fritz hadn't answered, I knelt, too.

Gallantly Dean positioned himself between me and the grisly scene that the flashlight had caught momentarily, before it dimmed again. But I'd already seen the long gash across the throat and the gray, bloody fur.

"Sick," Dean said wretchedly. "You gonna be okay, Mrs. Templeton? I'll . . . bury him for you."

But I couldn't release Fritz so easily. Gently, I moved Dean aside, gathered the furry, sticky mass into my arms, and allowed my tears to drop.

"Mrs. Templeton . . . please don't cry. Who coulda—"

I'd heard that same tone in his voice as he'd mourned his ruined mural. Dear Dean, to ache as deeply for my loss as for his own. Carefully, I laid the mutilated body in his arms.

"I'll find a nice, quiet spot," he promised. "I'll show you where later. Can you get home?"

"Yes," I said. I didn't need light. I was blinded by tears, anyway.

Because of my tears, the ineffectual streetlights, and my jumbled emotions, I stumbled many times during those final two blocks. If only Arden had been home. If only . . .

But no amount of wishing could bring Fritz back. Dear, faithful, loving Fritz. What possible reason could anyone have to harm him?

Yet I knew that in this town—which "made mincemeat of ministers," which had destroyed a young boy's mural, which allowed the park to be trampled for a carnival but denied children the right to play ball there . . . where someone could terrorize with telephone calls and effigies—there were several reasons I could name. And one of them was Turk.

And yet, if Turk had killed Fritz, wouldn't he have lurked nearby? Could he have passed up yet another opportunity for emotional violence?

Of course, Dean had been there with me. A witness.

But Dean wasn't with me now.

Arden, I thought. Arden, I need you.

"You've got to learn to lean on only one person," Dr. David had said. "Yourself. You're the only one you can *always* depend on to be available." (*Except for God*, I'd amended silently then. And added now.) I wondered how gentle Dr. David would have reacted to Fritz's lifeless body.

And I knew. He'd have been hurt and angry, as Dean was.

Warm light glowed from the parsonage. I was home.

Would McClintock ever, truly, feel like home? Surely never as the city church had—a place of sheltering, of nurturing. Of safety.

What had possessed Lelia to leave the front door hanging wide open like that, after dark?

I hurried up the front steps, into the living room. The television played, its artificial laughter responding to jokes spoken too softly for my hearing.

"Lelia?" I called, just as softly. "Pam?"

No answer. But once I'd turned off the TV, I could hear the rattle of water. Lelia had said that she planned a long, leisurely shower.

Had Pam opened the front door? A chill ran through me as I remembered that earlier evening when she'd come pattering back into the house with a cookie from an unknown benefactor.

"Pam!"

No answer. I felt panic gather. Mushroom. Multiply.

The rattle, the hammer of water continued. But why hadn't Pam answered?

Asleep. That was it. She was asleep.

Gasping, stumbling, I raced upstairs to her room.

Empty.

I hurried to the bathroom door, pounding, calling, crying. "Lelia!" The water pelted. "*Lelia?*"

I tried the door. The bathroom was empty, too. But why had she left the water running? A wet towel lay on the floor. My bathrobe was draped on a peg.

More to gain time and stabilize my thoughts than to conserve water, I turned off the spigots. Where *were* Pam and

Lelia? If only I could be certain they were together. But what if Lelia, showering, had thought Pam in danger? No matter how quickly she'd dressed, Pam could have been out of sight long before Lelia could react.

Oh, Arden . . . Arden, I need you.

The pattern of panic burgeoned. I sensed myself sinking to the bathroom floor, hugging the flashlight. Rocking, crying.

And what good could any of that do? If the person who'd killed Fritz so brutally had taken Pam . . .

Oh, Arden . . . oh, God. Please . . . please . . .

Useless grieving, Dr. David would have called it. And rightly so. Action first. *Then* leisure for tears.

Shouting Pam's name again, but no longer expecting response, I ran, slid, fumbled down the staircase.

The front door? I'd come in that way.

Then the kitchen. Yes, the kitchen.

Or the basement? Please—not the basement. The door was still locked, the chair in place. Thank God. Not the basement.

The back door stood open, too. And not only open, but sagging on its hinges, as though it had been wrenched.

And, on the back porch, one of Pam's little socks.

I picked it up. Held it to my face. Had Lelia seen it? Left it as a guide for me to follow? Or had she gone another direction entirely?

If only Fritz were there! But someone had removed Fritz from the picture. And Arden—everyone knew that Arden would be home late.

Turk knew.

Across the lawn I noticed a spot of comparative lightness. Why didn't the clouds dissipate? Why wouldn't the flashlight work? Why hadn't I thought to find fresh batteries?

I stooped. A hair ribbon.

And—yards beyond that—Pam's teddy bear.

What had it taken to separate her from her teddy? I paused, listening, waiting for her crying, however distant. I picked up the teddy, then threw it to the ground in horror. Its throat had been slashed, like Fritz's!

But teddy bears bleed only stuffing. Not blood, like Fritz. Like Pam. I heard my strangling sounds, my sobs, my wordless supplications to God, to Arden, to anyone. To . . . whoever it was who had Pam. *Please, please, don't hurt my baby.*

A rumpled something ahead. Another sock.

And beyond that . . .

The woods.

I was being led to the woods. Surely those signals weren't random. And Pam was too young to think of leaving a trail. Someone—someone who hated me—*wanted* me to follow. To the woods.

Inexplicably, I felt peace. *I* was the target. Surely I was the target, and Pam merely the bait. This person, Turk, whoever, didn't plan to hurt Pam. And yet . . . there was the grisly bundle that had once been vibrant Fritz.

Fritz could have sounded an alarm. And Pam . . . Pam could identify . . . whoever it was.

I'd gone full circle in my thinking, returning to blind panic. And I'd reached the woods.

Drawing a deep, trembling breath, I looked back toward the twinkling sanctuary of McClintock. The bulky stability of the housing development. Then, stepping carefully to avoid the treachery of unseen wire, I entered the deeper darkness.

Landmarks were camouflaged. I couldn't recognize the spot where the torn sketch had fluttered in the breeze. Still, the image flickered in my mind.

"Pam?" I called tentatively. No answer.

Where was I being led? Occasionally switching on the dim, dying flashlight, I peered about for signs. And found one. A string of plastic beads, laid like an arrow, pointing toward the stream.

Tripping over rocks, starting at sounds of scurrying creatures, flailing about for handholds, wincing from the slap of a briar across my cheek, I stumbled forward.

Oh, God, I prayed, *how much farther?*

And no one knew where I was. Or that I was even gone. And Arden would come home tired and unsuspecting.

I'd left no clues. I'd tucked Pam's little socks into my pocket. And the hair ribbon.

Dumb . . . dumb . . . dumb.

Dr. David would have had something to say about such self-assessment. But Dr. David was holding civilized conversation somewhere—*he* wasn't in a life-and-death struggle to save his child.

Save her?

How could I save her alone? And how could further help come when I'd left no sign?

Stupid . . . stupid . . . stupid.

I must stop wasting time and energy in foolish self-recrimination. I must plan what to do when I saw Pam, or heard her . . . when I'd identified the enemy.

But how could I plan when every strand of attention must go to staying on my feet?

A fallen limb turned under my shoe, and I thudded to the ground, both wrists twisting beneath me, the flashlight clattering away. Still, for a moment, I closed my eyes gratefully, gasped air that didn't move against me, and touched foliage that felt cool. Non-threatening.

When I opened my eyes, it was to a silvering of moonlight. *Thank you, God!*

Surely, somewhere ahead, Lelia was searching. Perhaps she'd already reached the end of the trail and waited only for my help.

I found the flashlight. Found my way to the stream. And to footprints—Lelia's? Too small to be Turk's, but leading toward Amy and Turk's special place, where, in happier days, they'd walked together.

CHAPTER 17

Strange, the deeper peace that enveloped me with the moonlight, the footprints, and the near-certainty of reaching my destination.

Peace? Or numbness?

Whichever, I regained the sense of control that I'd lost after beginning my search for Fritz.

Fritz. Dear Fritz. A sacrifice to someone's dislike for me.

Dislike? Too weak a word. Far, far too weak. Try loathing. Malice. Vengefulness. All too weak.

But I had to leave such thoughts, which could lead only to paralysis again. For Pam, for Lelia—and for myself—I needed mobility, both mental and physical.

And spiritual. Spiritual mobility? Was there such a thing? *Should* there be? Stability seemed better. God was stable. *Be with me, God. Be with Pam. With Lelia. With Arden, as he drives home through the moonlight. Does he sense that something's wrong? Let him drive safely. Let him know that I love him, even though I didn't tell him.*

Enough of that. Grieving dulls the senses.

A sound.

What?

The snap of a twig?

I paused. Listened, ears straining . . .

The sigh of breeze, almost infinitesimal. The murmur of the creek. Ahead, the muted growl of rapids. Only a purring, still too distant for the hiss and crash and thunder to threaten.

Except—perhaps they threatened Pam. And Lelia.

No time to listen for twigs. It could have been a deer passing.

The thought of a deer moving nearby brought comfort.

Or it might be the bear that I'd been told sometimes rummaged in the dump beyond the town.

Comfort fled. Though better the bear than Turk.

Please, God—will this never end?

Did I want to know its ending?

Thrusting my throbbing arms against low branches, lit by moonlight, I plunged headlong into briars that lashed and tore. No matter.

The rapids became living, heaving. Breathing violence.

"Pam? Lelia?" I paused. No answer.

Farther. Leaving the rapids behind, reduced to purring again. What had they said—Amy and Lelia? Next came the pool, and beyond that, more angry water. The gorge. The . . . swinging bridge.

Nausea rose in my throat. The bridge. I couldn't cross the bridge. I could never, ever, give myself to that height. That swaying.

Not even for Pam? For Lelia?

"We do what we must," Dr. David had said. "It's amazing, the courage we muster for those we love. Look what you've accomplished already! Trust yourself."

I could never, ever trust myself to a swaying bridge.

Then trust God.

It had been as clear as a voice. Arden's voice.

But Arden wasn't acrophobic. And Arden was off, somewhere, driving through moonlight. Perhaps whistling. Surely calm. Arden was always calm. I tasted resentment.

Better resentment than nausea.

Of course, God wasn't acrophobic either.

Thoughts churned, more loudly than the lapping of pooled water. But not more loudly than . . .

The laughter. Turk's laughter? Not his laughter of the kitchen, certainly. Of the living room.

This was the laughter I'd heard, over and over and over, on the telephone. And it was . . . where? I glanced all about. No one. Had there been a bulky shadow—moving away?

Away. I sighed with relief. Not closer, at least. Although closer, perhaps, to the bridge.

The swaying bridge. A hundred feet above the gorge. Isn't that what one of them had said? Amy? Or Lelia?

A hundred feet! When a stepladder, sturdy and metal, brought weakness. A hundred feet. And *swaying* . . .

I dropped to the ground, nearly retching. I couldn't!

We do what we must . . .

Shut up, Dr. David!

I scrambled to my feet.

"Lelia! Pam!" I called as I ran. As I stumbled. As I left the pool behind. Climbed. Heard the churning of the angry waters, and, cresting a slope, saw for the first time, delineated in the moonlight—the bridge.

Please, God—I can't.

We do what we must . . .

Paula is strong, Dr. Connelly. Strong . . .

Not strong.

I forced myself to move toward the bridge, one foot before another. One heavy, heavy, reluctant foot.

And stopped. There, just where the moorings of the bridge rose from rock—something, a crumpled shadow? Moving slightly.

"Pam?" I called softly. "Lelia?"

"Mrs. . . . Templeton," her voice said weakly. The shadow moved, gathering itself. Sank back. "Paula."

"*Lelia!*"

Even by the faint light of the moon I could see that her face was pale. She had slipped, she explained. Had turned her ankle. Had crawled—there, see where she'd dragged herself through leaves, through mud, across roots.

I touched her shoulder in sympathy, my glance darting here, searching there. "Pam?"

She sobbed. Pointed across the bridge.

Across the bridge! And Lelia unable to walk! And Arden still on the road.

Though perhaps, by now, he'd be at the parsonage, for all that helped, calling our names.

I didn't ask if it was Turk who had Pam. Better I not know. One thing at a time. First, the bridge.

I swallowed the bile rising in my throat. I would not vomit.

"You'll be all right?" I asked Lelia, my mind already on the bridge, swaying.

"Just . . . Pam . . ." There was wildness in her eyes.

As, I was sure, there was wildness in mine.

"I'm sorry," she whispered harshly.

"Sorry," I repeated, and bent to hug her. "Why should *you* be sorry? You've done so much for Pam. For all of us."

"I did—what I had to."

We do what we must. Dr. David's words—and an echo of Lelia's—got me onto the bridge. I clutched the side ropes against the swaying, moved my body forward, willing my feet to follow. My wrist sparked with pain. My knees gave way. I fell to them, moved forward on them. Retched. Vomited over the side of the bridge into the churning, thundering, glistening waters.

Knowing they waited for me, I stared into them. Shook myself loose.

Look up, I told myself. Look up. I will look unto the hills, from whence cometh my help . . . *help me, God.* I will look unto the clouds . . . help me, God.

The clouds, outlined by moonlight, were closing in, filming over.

And if the darkness came again . . .

At least darkness would hide the foaming waters, the remaining span of bridge. In darkness I could feel my way, feel the motion—but not see what occasioned it. Perhaps, the darkness would seem more friendly. Familiar. I could move by touch. By sound.

Sound . . .

Mingling with the sound of the water, of my breathing, of the scraping of my knees on roughness . . . the laughter.

Not from the far side of the bridge.

Behind me!

Why hadn't Lelia warned me?

And, with the mounting laughter, a stronger swaying. I knew that I must turn. Must see my enemy. But, just as I forced the muscles of my neck to yield, to move . . . the clouds extinguished all light from the moon.

CHAPTER 18

I peered into darkness but could see only that. Darkness, total and terrifying. Yet the heaving of the bridge and the rising laughter proved that the enemy who shared that dark, unstable space was close.

"Pam," I said, my voice croaking. Pleading.

And the laughter increased.

I tried to get to my feet. "*What have you done with Pam?*"

And the answer, still blended with laughter, came. "Pam was always safe."

I sank back in disbelief. My hands loosened on the ropes—then gripped again as the bridge lurched.

"*Lelia?*" I whispered. "But why?"

"You gave me the strength," she said, her voice her own. "I want to thank you for that."

"The strength?"

"To do what I had to do."

How different the context, then, of those once-reassuring words! "To . . . terrorize me?"

"To kill you," she said, without expression.

I sighed, strangely calm. At least Pam was safe. At least my mind needn't be torn in two directions. That is, if Lelia was telling the truth.

"Where *is* Pam?"

"With Grandmother. They think we're still looking for

Fritz." She added gently, "You should have known that I'd never hurt Pam. I *love* Pam!"

"I know that. But I don't understand—"

"You don't understand anything!" She chuckled. "That's what made it so easy! Just a simple telephone call—and you went to pieces. And the marigolds . . . and the dummy in the basement. I was watching. It was all I could do not to laugh out loud. How pale and stupid you were! Who else could it have been but me? Who else would have known where things were? But you never guessed—"

"And Fritz," I said coldly. "Fritz trusted you. He *loved* you!"

I heard her swift intake of breath. Felt a renewed swaying in the bridge. "It bothered you, didn't it," I asked softly. "Killing Fritz?"

She seemed in control again. "Certainly more than it will bother me to kill you. You think you're so brilliant. So sophisticated." Her voice was tinged with sarcasm. With superiority. "But you were much easier to fool than the others."

The others? But I didn't ask.

"I was in love with them, first. Long before you came here. And when Arden was so kind—I knew I loved him, too."

"You . . . loved *Arden*?"

She laughed again. "See how stupid you are? You never guessed! You thought I wanted to be *your* friend!"

"Perhaps it was only that you were so clever," I ventured, keeping my voice calm. My body still.

She lurched, setting the bridge into frantic motion. "Don't play games with me! You're so . . . so *transparent!*" She spat the word. "So weak! You don't deserve to be his wife. Or Pam's mother."

What now, God? I wondered. I might keep her talking.

But to what end? No one would be coming to help. I had only myself to depend on. Dr. David had been right.

"She loves me better," Lelia was saying comfortably. "Even you can see that."

"She loves you," I admitted, and heard her purring chuckle of victory. "But she'll hate you if you kill me."

"She'll never hate me. She'll never *know* I killed you."

I could sense her settling near me.

"It's going to be an accident. A terrible, tragic accident. And I'm going to blame myself for not leaving a note that I'd left Pam with Grandmother, while I went off in another direction, looking for Fritz."

"Dean and I found Fritz," I said levelly. "Dean will know that I wouldn't come out here again, searching—"

"Not for Fritz! You came looking for *Pam!*" She explained patiently, "Because I didn't realize you'd be back so soon, or I'd be so long, and I didn't leave the note." Her voice grew patronizing. "You've really got to listen more closely in the future," and she nearly choked on the laughter that followed.

"Lelia," I reached out to touch her, then thought better of it. "Lelia, I understand—some of the things you're feeling."

"Oh, yes!" she snapped. "You told me about your silly blackness! We have *nothing* in common, you and me," she snickered, "except for Pam. And the parsonage."

In an echo from the past, I heard Madge Pears saying comfortably, "This parsonage is like a second home to her." And Lelia herself had said that only the parsonage offered comfort.

"Just that in common," she was murmuring. "That, and of course Arden."

"What makes you think he'll love you?" I sneered. "Rev. Winters didn't. And Rev. Martin—"

I'd caught her off-guard, but too harshly. Dangerously.

Her hands fastened on my wrists, already pounding with pain. Shaking me roughly, she sobbed, "Andy was *beginning* to love me! He *was*! And then they found my letters and sent him away—"

She rocked back and forth, her hair brushing my cheek, her tears wetting my neck. "Both of them needed me," she said more steadily. "They told me so, over and over. 'What would we do without you, Lelia?' they'd ask, and 'God sent you to us,' they'd say. But Rev. Winters treated me like a daughter—patting my head or my shoulder. His real caresses went to that shell of a wife. The way he looked at her . . . I knew he'd have to go. So easy, anyway, with Minnie Kelp insisting we needed someone who'd give his whole attention to church affairs. If only Mrs. Winters had died . . . . " Her voice strengthened. "But Andy had seen me as a lover—or would have . . . soon."

I found myself wanting to comfort her as I'd have comforted Pam. "Oh, Lelia."

She stiffened. "Don't pity me! *You're* the one everyone'll pity. Except for Minnie Kelp, of course. And Turk. They'll be glad you're dead. And so will I. No one will guess, though. I'll cry for a while, and say I'm to blame. And they'll comfort me, just as they did when Mrs. Winters had her stroke." She laughed deeply, and I knew without having to be told that somehow she had induced it— "Then, gradually, we'll all forget." She paused, and finished spitefully. "Pam will forget the easiest of all."

She was right, of course. At first, Pam would grieve. But soon I'd become fuzzy in her young memory, and, eventually, I'd be only a photograph.

I slumped with weariness. It was obvious that nothing I could say would have power over Lelia. Her hatred, her madness were too deep. If only I could summon an equal hatred, perhaps I'd have some chance in the struggle that must come. The sooner the better, I thought, startling myself. Had Mrs. Winters, too, yearned for a conclusion as Lelia exposed her true feelings, as shock surged through aging blood vessels? Even as revulsion caught at her breath and congealed speech and movement, had she known hatred for this young woman whose softness masked cunning?

But I couldn't hate Lelia! I'd spent too many months locked in my own blackness, afraid of my own potential for violence, to despise someone else who was trapped. Fearful. Yearning.

Unexpectedly, she said, "I'm really sorry I have to do this." And I believed her. "At first," she admitted softly, "I just wanted them to think you were crazy again. To shut you away. But this is better. This is . . . final." She sighed, and I sensed that the moment had come.

Wordlessly, I raised my mind to God. And my prayer was for Lelia as well.

Deliberately, steadily, she stood and pulled me with her. The bridge wavered, and I fell to my knees again.

"Stand up," she whispered harshly. "Stand up!" Hooking her thumbs near my ears, she forced my chin upward with the palms of her hands.

Suddenly, the clouds slipped away from the moon, and I saw her face close above me, its features altered by shadows. I could hear the harshness of her breath, struggling, as her hands forced me back . . . back. Rope scraped, searing me from shoulder blade to waist as the bulk of her body pressured me toward space. Toward death.

Forget the lurching bridge. Forget everything but Pam. Arden. Life . . .

Heaving upward with my knee, I caught her in the soft flesh of her stomach. Gasping, she relaxed her grip.

Scrambling for equilibrium, I burned my palms as I

dragged myself to the comparative stability of the swaying bridge floor.

She groped for my throat, digging her thumbnail into its base, pressing downward, but having a greater mobility in my squat position, I squirmed to one side. She cursed, slapping viciously, but delivering only a glancing blow.

The force of her movement threw her heavily to one side, and it was she, suddenly, against the ropes, then down. And I was grabbing, clutching, scrambling to achieve the upper position.

Crazily, the bridge pitched. Quivered. Writhed. Grimly, I steadied myself by a handhold of Lelia's hair—and she struggled, puffed, cursed beneath me.

She was so *strong*! Stronger, by far, than I. *Paula is strong, Dr. Connelly* . . .

Not strong enough! Inexorably, Lelia was freeing herself, forcing me over the edge once more, and I knew that this time would be the last; there was in her every movement a determination and a power I could never match.

I kicked. I scratched. I butted my head into her belly, her breast—and she went down. Hard. The bridge swung wildly until I thought it must turn over, spilling us both into the churning water.

But my fear of the height, of the movement, was gone, superseded by the fear of dying here. Of abandoning Pam. Of leaving Arden without assuring him of my love.

She lay, unmoving. I wanted to touch her. To speak her name . . . but I couldn't trust her. She might be waiting there, hoping I'd be so foolish.

Slowly, I stepped backward. Toward the unexplored shore. Step by swaying step. Feeling my way with my feet, with my hands on the ropes.

And she stirred.

Turning, then, I ran as swiftly as the uncertain footing

would permit. Rocks lay close enough that moonlight high-lighted edges and cast crevices into deep shadow. Then, just as one foot touched solid ground, Lelia caught my ankle, throwing me face-first to hard earth and leaf-mold. I kicked back, hard, felt her release, heard the breath knocked from her. I scrambled to my feet and stumbled toward shadows, just as clouds covered the moon once more and the whole world became shadow.

I heard her standing, catching her breath. I sensed her listening, ready to respond to any small movement.

I felt for a pebble, tossed it as far away as I could, and heard her scornful laughter. And under the shelter of that rising sound, I eased away and sought sanctuary near the arching, exposed roots of a giant tree.

"Mrs. *Temp*-le-ton," she called softly.

I shuddered.

Perhaps she'd caught even that small stirring. I could hear her moving my way. Then in another direction. I wanted to sigh with relief, but held my breathing carefully in check.

"Mrs. *Temp*-le-ton." How much more terrifying, that softened, singsong tone! "Come out, come out, wherever you are." Like a child, playing a game.

My nerves quivered.

"Feel the blackness, Paula. Remember how the black-ness frightens you."

Obviously, she was trying to elicit some sign of fractur-ing. Stiffening, I felt the vibration of muscle; the need of ten-don to stretch; a desperation for flight, away from this danger, away from her, to light. To Arden. To safety. But I denied myself movement.

"I've had enough of this, haven't you?"

Yes, each nerve answered. *Yes!*

"Why don't you come out and we'll . . . talk." Only her low laughter robbed her words of normalcy.

"I know where you are."

I drew a long, quivering breath.

And she moved—not toward me, but away from me. Toward the bridge? Straining my ears, I reached through the darkness. No! To one side of the bridge! Surely toward the chasm. Toward the murderous waters.

Standing, forgetting my own jeopardy, I screamed her name in warning.

Too late.

The grating, the sliding, the crashing of rocks told me that—and her sharp, unbelieving scream that echoed and echoed, long after the small avalanche had stilled, long after the roar of water had covered her actual cry.

By then, the moon had freed itself once more. Too late to save Lelia, but in time to illuminate my leaden return across the bridge, which could hold no terror or horror to match the thought of Lelia's body, lying shattered below.

CHAPTER 19

The bridge swayed beneath me, its splintery planks snagging the soles of my shoes.

I'd lost the flashlight. No matter. In a night of such major losses, flashlights were easily expendable.

At times the moon washed the downward path in liquid light. Silvered each drooping branch and its layered foliage. Glinted on blades of grass, on needles of pine and hemlock. Discovered the mica in pathside rocks. Another time, I'd have admired its beauty, have yearned to commit it to canvas. Now, my numbed perceptions could have been viewing another world altogether. When the moon hid, periodically, the blackness felt more familiar. Almost welcoming.

Gradually, the thunder of the rapids receded to murmuring. To whispering. To silence broken only by my padded footfalls and the occasional creaking of a branch. Once, an owl hooted. Something heavy moved through underbrush. I was indifferent. Natural threats couldn't compare with what I had already faced.

I felt my way toward thinning woods. Stepped carefully where wire coiled. Paused, whispering a jumbled prayer, at the crest near the housing complex. And then, in headlong flight born both of relief and of panic, I stumbled toward home.

It was only when I reached the back porch steps, only

when I'd called Pam's name, that I gave myself gladly to comforting, sinking darkness.

The couch, our blue couch, was soft beneath me, our living room was warm with light. And Arden was there. Arden.

I reached out, then tried to sit up. "Pam!"

"She's here," several voices assured me. "She's safe."

She was always safe, I remembered. And sighed.

"Don't think about it now," urged Arden, kneeling beside me, stroking my forehead. His eyes were warm. Loving.

But I *had* to think about it! Before I could put that night's terror behind me, I must tell him . . . tell them? . . . its greatest horror.

"Lelia," I whispered, and felt tears sliding down my cheeks.

"What about Lelia?" I saw Madge standing behind Arden's shoulder, and beyond her, Dora and Skinny.

"Oh, Madge! There was an accident. A terrible accident. Lelia . . . the bridge . . ."

She drew a long sigh. "Then she's dead?"

I nodded.

"Well," and her voice shook only a little, "she had always rather been dead."

But even through my tears I saw the starkness of her expression as Dora enclosed her and led her away.

CHAPTER 20

It had been a tragedy, everyone agreed.

In a poignant tribute in *The Danvers Bugle,* Mary Lynn Whitman wrote that for Lelia to venture so far at night to search for a lost dog showed the depth of her compassion and the intensity of her love for her new friends. Her death was a loss to the whole community, one which underscored the fragility of life. The need to get along with one another, in forbearance and in love.

Even Minnie Kelp echoed that sentiment as she apologized, though a bit stiffly, to Dean at the arts-and-crafts show Dee and I engineered late in the summer.

Minnie still wasn't speaking to me. Perhaps later, in a year or two, she could bring herself to. But she was attending church again, and she had helped to prepare refreshments for Angie and Ted's wedding reception.

Amy returned for the wedding. Surprisingly, Turk hung quietly on the edges of the festivities, approaching her only as she left, when he opened her car door and shut it gently behind her, then watched, hands in his pockets, as she drove away. I had seen Turk only twice since the night of Lelia's death, and he'd carefully avoided eye contact.

"He'd better," Arden had growled, when I'd explained the bruises on my wrist. And yet Turk had been openly vicious, while Lelia—

Lelia had been ill. Nothing could convince me that the

coldly calculating side of her character was dominant. How often I'd witnessed the warmth, the yearning, even gratitude, and known them genuine. Poor wounded child! Lifelong loss had soured and warped her.

Perhaps Turk's loss of Amy would alter him for the better.

"Perhaps," Arden agreed, but with a curl of his lip.

In the flush of humanity that warmed the whole community, at least for a while, Arden was informed that the boys might, after all, practice baseball in the park, since "they probably wouldn't do much more damage than the crowds did during carnival week."

In the basement of the East Danvers church, Dean and his co-workers had equalled—perhaps even surpassed—the mural that had once embellished the wall where Great-aunt Alice's "Last Supper" once again hung in its place of honor.

Perhaps that, too, in time might be replaced.

But we weren't expecting too much. Dr. Connelly warned us not to, even as he breathed a sigh of deep relief—and gratitude?—when we told him that yes, Arden would accept an extension of his appointment at McClintock.

He'd cleared his throat. "A tragedy often has a softening, gathering-together effect for a time. But the McClintock charge, I'm afraid, will always be a challenging one. Who knows, it may still take a church fight to clear the air. But you'll be long-gone before that."

Perhaps.

Yet, more and more, McClintock feels like home, and never more so than when we visit the peaceful spot where Dean buried Fritz. Or when Pam solemnly pats the mounded turf of another, larger grave, and we speak gently of a friend who is gone.

Arden is the only other person who knows what really happened that night on the bridge. Whether rightly or wrongly, we decided that no good purpose could be served by tarnishing Lelia's memory. And Dean has long since decided that Fritz was killed by some cruel transient, that no one in McClintock could be capable of such an act.

And I?

Whenever I recall those days of fear and terror, I simply thank God that the darkness is ended at last.